T0146916

THE
Cerebral Maze

Jessica Yellowknife

Order this book online at www.trafford.com
or email orders@trafford.com

Most Trafford titles are also available at major online book retailers.

Printed in the United States of America.

ISBN: 978-1-4907-0580-4 (sc)
ISBN: 978-1-4907-0581-1 (e)

Trafford rev. 07/24/2013

 www.trafford.com

North America & international
toll-free: 1 888 232 4444 (USA & Canada)
fax: 812 355 4082

I dedicate this book to
Mildred Jacquith-Broadbent, 1998.

Prologue

She was experiencing the nightmares again. It seemed now, to be occurring nightly on a regular basis. Restlessly, she moved to a different position on her firm army bed. Nothing seemed to help. She just couldn't fall asleep. Stress, fatigue or something deeper . . . Disturbing thoughts seemed to be overflowing through her mind. Shivering, she pulled up the thick, green blanket. It was such a coarse material, not comfortable in the least. Rotating around once more, she nudged her pillow off her cot. Her army cot was basically just a small collapsible bed. Reaching down, she picked up the pillow and shoved it back under her head. Glancing upwards, she tried to pierce to darkness of the tent, but was unable to.

Her sleeping and working area wasn't one of any magnitude. There was barely enough room to sleep in, let alone work in. The tiny work area consisted of a brown folding wooden table and a torn leather chair. Located on top of the table as a Hewlett Packard laptop computer, an HP printer and a pile of rolled up geological maps and documents? With her work space so limited, she often used her army cot as an extra work area to prepare her maps and reports for her clients.

They were starting to prove to be quite hostile people to work for. Preparing herself for an emergency escape, she continually backed up all her results into her powerful laptop computer. She was a guest in a large and powerful country. Now she was starting to regret her invitation to work for these people. *To hell with his payment for the job, she thought, the results intended just weren't showing up.* If she did have to leave quickly, she intended to better analyze the results elsewhere. She wanted somewhere safe, where she could prepare the final report without getting her neck slit while she slept. She would send them all the results later; it didn't pay to make enemies with these people.

Really cold in here, she thought. Normally temperatures, hot and cold, didn't bother her. Since she had started working here, she had been experiencing occurring nightmares. Like a cold winter wave splashing against a rough shoreline, she experienced icy droplets of sweat dripping down her forehead upon wakening up.

The dream was always the same, but lately it seemed to be intensified. It was severely jarring her mind. Rising up from the cot, her body reacted with a tremor like effect. Dreams flowed through her mind about a dangerous area of frozen glaciers, icebergs and a steep mountainous terrain.

She experienced visions of cold, constantly blowing winds blasting through days that consisted of no darkness. As she woke up in the cold room, the temperature around her seemed to stimulate her in ways she hadn't felt before. Was it the cold, or the fact that she had no memories of her youth . . . ?

It had been years ago, but clinically she had been declared brain dead for almost a minute . . . The doctors had resurrected her, and later she had revived after suffering a six month coma. Upon awakening in the strange hospital room, at the age of seventeen, she found that life had now changed for her. Her right eye was heavily bandaged, and her memories of her past were gone. This was why the nightly dreams caused her concern. Was it just a nightmare, or were memories of her youth starting to come back to her? She could remember everything from the age of seventeen. Anything before that time period was a blur.

The day had been long and tedious, definitely not one of her better exploration projects. Every morning, she was always up before sunrise. She didn't want her clients to catch her sleeping's the people who respected the darkness before sunrise, had worked the long, hard hours outdoors all day. Following supper came more hours of taking her clients work results and plotting them down on various maps. Then came the studying of what her results meant. Each report had to be hand written, as to her recommendations for the next days work. She was careful to add all of the results, along with her daily journal onto her laptop.

Exhaustion was setting in. Work had continued on like this for a month straight with no breaks. Slowly, the tossing around on the bed stopped. She started to nod off. The raised cot felt more comfortable now. She slept until early morning, when the nightmare began again. This time it was much more unsettling. Blackness overcame her. She was now experiencing the outer limits of her mind, as she penetrated through the freezing icy cold winds, entering a dark log cabin, and encountering someone called the Female Suffrage.

Darkness and eerie was the atmosphere that prevailed in the Female Suffrage's roughly hewn log cabin. It was lit by only a single oil burning lamp. A sweet yet pungent aroma of burning incense sticks flickered upwards. It blended with the smoke of a rich aromatic cigar that the Female Suffrage was smoking.

In the center of the room was a large table, made with the wooden remnants of an old shipwreck. The wreckage had been found perfectly preserved on the shoreline of Baffin Island. It had been partially submerged in the cold waters of the Nacres Strait which separated Baffin Island from Greenland. As the freezing water had flowed over the wooden shipwreck it had preserved the wood and given it a unique appearance. The table's legs were made of carved whale bone. In the middle of the table was a massive piece of thick, furry seal skin with a huge burning oil lamp set upon it. The table was a marvellous piece of ingenuity. It was handmade by a local tribe of aboriginal Indians who lived in Paginating by the Cumberland Sound on the Northern tip of Baffin Island. This Aboriginal Indian tribe had survived all their lives nearly forty miles from the Arctic Circle. Their environment had some of the harshest conditions for existence found anywhere.

The Female Suffrage had been well pleased with this gift made specifically for the Female Suffrage's Cabin. It was their gift of honouring her and the inauguration of Canada's second most Northerly Park. She had made it a point to have food and supplies sent out to this tribe twice a year to help them survive out in their rugged surroundings.

The presided Female Suffrage at the head of the table seated on a deep chair covered with a rich purple velvet cloth. She wore a matching set of purple velvet pyjamas and a purple velvet robe. On her left hand as a ring with an Amethyst jewel. The Female Suffrage had very few changeable habits, but one of them was her fondness for one colour one time and perhaps a different one later. Just now she was experiencing a yen for purple, particularly the regal shade of the colour.

The woman could go in for colors like a female movie star, and still be dangerous. She did not look dangerous as she glanced around the room; the Female Suffrage never looked dangerous.

Seated at the table, on antique chairs were fourteen young ladies crouched down listening attentively, as the Female Suffrage discussed her plans. A terrified uneasiness jumped over the faces of the young ladies as she discussed her plans for them. It was a tribute to the grisly qualities of the innocent looking, tall, thin women before them.

Something hypnotic was seen in all of her carefully planned moves. She had not raised her voice or touched them, yet they all shrank backwards into their chairs. The Female Suffrage was through. Attention to detail, she had long ago learned was most important. Overlook a seed, and it may grow into a great tree of thorns.

Two of the girls raised themselves up from their chairs. The smaller of the two youths asked. *"What the hell time is it?"* With a thin piercing glance of her eyes, the Female Suffrage examined an old fashioned time piece tucked into her purple waistband. *"Twelve AM."* She stated. Yet as she said it, she removed two large, beautifully crafted wooden boxes from an old wooden crate. Carefully, she placed them on the floor. Her eyes burned with a hypnotic glare, and her soothing but threatening voice burned into the large Canadian girl and the small, thin girl standing next to her.

They both walked over to the wall and pulled back the sealskin curtain which covered one of the four windows. The walls had darkened overtime with the constantly lit stove pipe oven emitting black smog. It had discoloured the walls with a permanently black distressed appearance.

The large youth pulled back the curtain and glanced out the window. A light from the window beamed into the dark cabin revealing a beautiful bright outdoor winter scene of glaciers and rugged nearby mountains. *"Damn Sunlight."* The large youth muttered.

"I take personal offence to the comment!" The women known as the Female Suffrage stated. "You *are in Baffin Island Park . . . soon to be known as Auyuittuq National Park Reserve . . . if I have anything to do with it. Further more the sun does not go down during the summer months in the Arctic Circle."*

With an innocent look, the Female Suffrage hissed out.*" You are guests in my cabin and you will cease your pacing and sit down with my other distinguished ladies."* Beads of fear started running down the faces of the two Canadian girls. Both quickly offered their apologies and sat down amongst the twelve other youths.

They had all been gathered together from an orphanage in a touch area of the Northern part of Toronto, Ontario. As the large youth sat down, she looked over at two stocky Asian girls. The Female Suffrage proceeded to take out twelve boxes. She placed them on top of the table in front of the twelve girls who had remained seated. From the floor she reached down and picked up the two remaining boxes. Slowly, she placed them with extreme care in front of the girls who had stood up during her meeting.

"You both have disappointed me!" The Female Suffrage banged her fist hard on her leg. *"I had my plans set for fourteen girls, which included my two Captains here."* An extended, narrow finger pointed out a petty aboriginal Indian girl with long black hair and a curved beak of a nose and at a blond haired youth with scars on her face seated next to each other. *"Now my plans will have to be altered. Instead of the fourteen working for me, there will now be ten."*

"Well plans do change!" The Female Suffrage soothed softly. *"My captains will now have seven operatives working for them instead of nine."* Contemplating, she glanced around the table. She stared into the eye of the young ladies as if reading their thoughts and receiving impressions of them. Reaching over with a few decision, she switched three of the boxes that the young ladies had in front of them with new ones from the other girls. *"You three will report directly to me, checking on the progress of the seven other girls and about the activities of my two Captains."*

"Now open your boxes and begin your futures." The Female Suffrage stated, letting her breath out slowly.

With a satisfied look, she watched as the ladies slowly opened their boxes. The two youthful Captains opened their boxes quickly as the other girls peeked over to see what was inside the beautifully crafted boxes were gleaming two inch peridot balls, set carefully into leather setting to hold them in place. The peridot balls had raised impressions of the world worked onto them. A gleaming Rudy jewel was set near the top of what they imagined to be the location of where they were all now located.

The next seven ladies opened their boxes and each found a shiny moonstone two inch ball with the same patterns but with an Onyx jewel instead. As the Female Suffrage watched with pleasure, the remaining three other ladies opened their boxes. The large Canadian youth looked at her smaller friend. They locked eyes while the large Canadian girl glanced down at her box, and motioned with her nose towards the large oil lamp located on the center of the table. Both firmly gripped their boxes as if to open them.

The last three ladies, who were to report directly to the Female Suffrage, found that they had similar balls, but of a oval bronzita with a glass poppy jasper jewel set on the top. Just as they were opening their boxes, the petty Canadian girl and her small friend shoved with all their might their boxes directly towards the large oil lamp which rested on the seal skin rug covering most of the table. As both boxes crashed into the oil lamp, the lamp fell over spilling oil onto the rug starting a smoky fire. The petty Canadian girl had suspected from the careful placement of the boxes in front of them that heir's had contained something that had to be handled carefully.

As the boxes crashed into the oil lamp starting a blazing fire, the two boxes both gave off a small explosion. The boxes when opened had been intended to explode into the two youths faces possibly killing them. The smoke was all over the room by now. The smaller youth felt her tugged out of the chair and pulled towards the door. The petty youth had placed the location in her mind's eye for the mad dash outside. *"Put out the fire, and then we'll deal with them."* The innocent look was gone. In the dark smoky room, her visage had finally taken on a dangerous appearance.

Containing the fire proved more difficult than first thought. The darkness, along with the smoke was hindering their efforts. The fire continued to push on despite of the efforts of the twelve ladies frantically trying to locate something in the darkness to put out the fire. Finally they opened the curtains, and with the use of their jackets pounding the flames on the table, the fire was put out. The smoke slowly dissipated throughout the room.

The Female Suffrage lined them up and shoved new outfits at them. She shouted out. *"Find them, and kill them, do it whatever way you feel like . . . . just make it painful."* Rushing out the door like a pack of hounds, the youths followed the two girl's trail which headed off towards the South. After ten minutes of following the trail, it completely disappeared. Where were they? The argument continued past fifteen minutes. They were bewildered and angry. Each headed off in their own separate direction. No trace was ever found of what had become of the petty Canadian girl and her smaller friend. They had simply vanished.

The Female Suffrage was angry. She spent months out in the frozen wasteland trying to find them. She spoke to the Aboriginal Indians who was in their little tent village. Had they ever seen them, but they spoke in their language that no strangers had ever approached their village. With rage unbecoming her, the Female Suffrage screamed out loud for ten minutes. She would find them. If it took her entire life to make them scream in misery, so be it. After that, she left and never sent supplies to the village again. Inside the cold igloo, the petty Canadian girl and her smaller friend shook with the coldness and the screams they heard outside.

*   *   *

With the coldness, the nightmare faded. It had been the most terrible and realistic dream she had experienced yet. *Was it her in the dream, she wondered.* She rubbed her black eye patch. So cold, she wrapped the blanket around her in a tired and dazed feeling. She stood up on the floor wondering where she as. As she walked across the sandy floor of the tent she could see the light becoming brighter with the mornings' sunrise. She shook off her tiredness and opened the front canopy of the tent door and looked outside.

It all came back to her now, as she woke up. Now she knew where she was. She looked around at the sun rising over the huge sand dunes. She dropped the blanket in amazement, remembering that she was here working in an oil exploration project in Saudi Arabia.

Soon, very soon, she would be sweating and baking under the immense heat of the Arabian Desert.

CHAPTER ONE

Elliot Lake, Ontario, Canada- Morning, January 11, 2013

A golden sunrise was slowly ascending. Softly, a glow appeared rising over the flat, snow covered roof of the semi-dark entranceway of the Bon Air Motel. Weather, forecasted for the day appeared to be unpredictable. One local TV channel predicted a decrease in the amount of snowfall that had occurred over the last two days. Yet, the radio station announced chances of warm spells followed by cold air patterns and possibly more snow.

Elliot Lake, a small mining town in Northern, Canada was experiencing a season of unusual precipitation in the form of days of unrelenting snowfall. Today the sky was clouding up the East, while the morning sun tried to fight its way through a scattering of grey clouds to the west. A cold, yet gentle wind was calmly scattering loose snow along the hard-packed snow of the Motels parking lot.

Ruth Tanner departed her Motel room. It was situated at the westerly corner of the Bon Air Motel. She was preparing herself mentally. Today, she would have to exert a lot of effort on performing out-of-the-ordinary

1

physical work. She looked around at the new fallen snow covering the cars in the parking lot. With a few hours driving, she would arrive at her Lachaise Property. It was situated to the south of Elliot Lake, and was a deeply wooded forest filled with a challenging snow filled rugged terrain. It was one of the many properties in the area that she owned the mining rights to.

She let out a short yawn, and pulled out a Colt Cigar, *Damn things she thought, I like them, but I can't seen to quit the habit.* Ruth pulled out a small pair of scissors from the pockets of her green hydro line jacket and clipped the end of the cigar. It seemed to make her happy that she wouldn't be smoking a full cigar.

Disgustedly, she looked at the battered up blue Chevy pickup truck, with its rust patches and matching holes that she had purchased with a small amount of cash. On the back sat a red powerful Summit HM ski-duo. Ruth Tanner did lots of rough outdoor work around the world, but she enjoyed mainly working in the winter in Northern Canada. Her world wide Geological Exploration Company was well known to produce results for its clients. Although it was probably one of the best exploration companies for gold, oil and precious minerals, it tended to be quite private. She preferred it to cater only to projects the Ruth found to be difficult and demanding.

The BRP Company, which made ski-duos, jet boats, all—terrain vehicles and much, had asked her to test out under the harshest conditions possible each of their newest line of up-coming 2013 models. The company specialized in many products, but they especially wanted her output on their newest line of ski-duos. They had delivered one of each of the new 2013 line of ski-duos for her to test while she was working in Elliot Lake. When she had the time she report back to them on how each handle in the varieties of harsh weather and working conditions the she specialized in.

It was cold out and the battery shook a little on the pickup before it kicked into life. Well, the pickup may be ugly, but this morning it started out smoothly with a minus 40 Fahrenheit weather temperature outside.

Ruth pushed in the clutch and headed down the back roads of Elliot Lake small town was located in the far northern part of Ontario, Canada. The roads were plowed but felt slippery today. She didn't take it as a good luck symbol. Sometimes she felt that she just worried too much. She had the ski-duo if the pickup went off the road. At least she wouldn't have to walk back the ten miles to town. It was nearing 6.30 AM as she pulled up to a pile of snow five feet high. Going through it was a freshly covered up snowmobile trail.

Parking the pickup, Ruth headed out towards the back and slammed down the tail gate. That felt good she thought as she started wondering about the change in the weather. It felt warmer she thought. She yanked on the end grip of the Ski-duo and hauled it off quickly. Ruth watched it bang down hard on the icy road. *Not my ski-duo she figured what the hell.* The large company had told her to test it any way she felt. It landed hard, but the powerful shock absorbers prevented any damage. Impressive she thought, I must mention that to them. Seating herself on its back sent she pushed the gas compressor button a couple of times and then pulled hard on the cord and heard the ski-duo's powerful motor roar to life.

Ruth wasn't a big girl, she was about 5 feet 1 inches tall, but she was exceptionally strong. She worked out at any gym that she could find in the towns that she worked in. Her biceps were huge; she had a powerful chest, waist and she was physically well devoted all over. She was a woman who kept to herself. A loner, she found that she seldom enjoyed the company of people. Sometimes she would talk to people as she did power lifting at the gym. Often when working out at the local martial arts club she would get into discussions with fellow martial artists. When necessary she discussed new geology technology and projects with other professional geologists.

Ruth allowed herself few pleasures. One of her past times was playing the stock market in new geological projects. She also enjoyed gambling at Roulette Tables at local Casinos and playing pool. She adored and was fascinated by the study of math. She enjoyed anything that was related to math. Ruth past-time and enjoyment was figuring out the odds at the Casinos, the angles in pool and the mathematical statistics at the stock market. These were some of the pleasures that she allowed herself. She could well afford it. She had her own company. She owned millions of dollars, some legal and some obtained through other means. Money meant nothing to her, except that it allowed her the freedom to travel around the world discovering and exploring various types of geological formations. Her hair was long in length and various shades of black and smoothly combed back. Her eyes were a golden brown that sparkle when they hit the light. Men found her to be quite attractive, but for some she kept her distance from them. Ruth usually wore dark sunglasses to hide the fact that she only had one eye. The right eye contained a glass eye but over the years she had adjusted to wearing it so that it didn't bother her.

As stood up on the Summit HM ski-duo, absorbing the outdoor pristine wilderness as winter was involving, she wondered what she had done to deserve the false eye. At seventeen years old, she had woken up to find she had been in a coma for six months. The authorities came by the next day to question her about her connection in a local murder investigation. It seemed that plenty of witnesses had seen her kill a local citizen in the worst possible condition. The police had pounded her with questions, but she couldn't remember anything previous to the coma no matter how hard she tried. She couldn't remember doing anything wrong. Her thinking was that she must have been guilty what with all the evidence and witnesses that had been brought up against her.

After psychiatric examinations and months of court appearances for her crime, she was taken to Kingston Woman Penitentiary. This was one of Ontario's oldest and toughest jails. Being one of the youngest members of Kingston Woman Penitentiary hadn't been easy. As the years went by, she had learned to handle her way around the jail. Fear had toughened her. She wasn't going to be anyone's play toy. She had proven her strength and lack of fear to bigger and tougher women on many occasions.

After three years of being in jail, her health suddenly began to deteriorate. Ruth began suffering extreme head pains, dizziness and blackouts.

Her cell mate was an old timer, named Susan gardener. She was locked away indefinitely for her life of crime. Susan had taken a liking to young Ruth and protected her during her period of poor health. Each night she would discuss how she had performed various crimes and how she had accomplished them. Proudly, she taught Ruth how to accomplish various act of thievery and introduced her to women in her line of work. During Susan's nightly stories of her past, Ruth never interrupted, even though she had heard each of them probably a hundred times.

Ruth's severe headaches worsened and she as brought to the jail hospital enfermería where she was informed that she was suffering from physical problems from her past. Her health problems were probably being brought on by the blow to the right side of her head and having her eye gauged out. It was assumed that a peridot ball with a ruby jewel on the side had been used to perform the rough surgery since it had been found next to Ruth's unconscious body. Unfortunately, for the person who had performed the violent act, she had dropped it near Ruth's body and forgotten it as she left Ruth for dead. Strangely, the Authorities had allowed her to keep the peridot ball until she went to jail. From there it was taken away and stored for safe keeping until she was released. The extreme trauma she had endured was catching up to her slowly.

She was told by Doctor that she would probably suffer physical or mental problems later. Between the hospital staff there had been much discussion on the possibility of lateral developing split personalities. Susan who at that time was around seventy years old and not likely to get out let Ruth know that she had no family and no outside friends. She discussed with Ruth the money she had hidden around the country. Susan told Ruth that if she got out of jail she could have all of the money to get her started back into a new life. She asked Ruth one thing in exchange, that she adopted her name when she felt a change coming over her.

To Susan way of thought, it felt like she could still continue the life that she had led since she was about Ruth's age. Slowly, Ruth health began to improve but unfortunately Susan died about six months later.

Surprisingly one day Ruth was released after serving four years in jail. New evidence had been brought up on her case. Some unknown person was helping her on the outside to clear her name. *Why someone would help me get out of jail, for a crime that she wasn't sure that she hadn't committed, she thought.* Later, she was proven innocent of the crime that the jury had pronounced on her. Ruth never found out who had helped her get out of the prison system but she was thankful for the assistance. It had even gone further in that the unknown individual had made sure that compensation was rewarded to her serving the lengthy time unjustly.

With the help of the financial assistance, Ruth went on to graduate with honours' at Cambrian College in Geological Exploration Technology. She had specialized in mining, mineral identification and geological formations around the world. After College Ruth went on to Laurentian University and got her Bachelor Degree in Business Geology. She had kept to herself. Ruth tended to be a loner with no friends or boys that interested her. She worked out continuously in the gym. She developed a strong and muscular body. To keep busy she tended to visit any local or out of town martial arts club and learn what she could about fighting. She studied everything she could about the various forms of self defence.

Ruth had been given back the heavy peridot ball by the Prison Administrator when she was released from jail. With danger in her heart, she had decided to make a weapon out of it. She had strapped the heavy peridot ball inside strong thinly cut braided strips of leather. On the end she formed a six inch braided leather handle. It also had a braided leather loop on the other end. Inside it was hollow, and she had inserted a strong spring inside the handle which worked two ways. With a flick the covered ball would eject itself from its' leather covered handle and by twisting her wrist Ruth could make the heavy covered ball soar six feet outward. It would then return by force to her. She could pull the loop at the other end of the handle, and two more feet of braided leather could be pulled out. She could strangle a woman to death with it easily. The weapon made also just for a simple club.

Everyday she practiced with it. Soon she found that she could do almost anything with her leather club. To avoid problems, instead of hanging it from her belt, she would simply put it through her belt pant loops and put the strap over the ball to tie the ends together. It made a beautiful, creative belt. Every time she went through airport security systems it world set off the alarms, but they had always let her through thinking it just another fancy belt buckle.

During College Ruth took Susan's considerable hidden patches of stolen money and invested it in the Stock Market. She became so good at it that by the end of College she was a Millionaire.

During University, she started up an unknown company gathering up geological information about mining and mineral exploration around the world. She set up the business in a large decrepit warehouse on the East side of Newfoundland, Canada. The building had once been a fish processing plant. Ruth then hired professional geologists who had become handicapped during their rugged work in which they had no benefit packages to assist them once they were hurt. She paid them extremely well and they enjoy continuing the work that they loved. Ruth had the old building renovated inside all the modern equipment to help them in their daily lives. Outside her kept the building looking run down and out of business. She put the geologist in charge of running the company. Ruth then had them gathering geological information from around the world. The information was then put on the latest computers. She didn't spare any money and made sure that they used the most up to date technology available.

Ruth then had access to geological information that no one else knew about. The company had spent four years gathering geological information from around the world. After completing her University degree, Ruth then opened up a legitimate company doing geological exploration around the world.

Around this time, Ruth started suffering changes in her personality. She became Susan Gardener the thief. She began pulling off criminal jobs, and adding more money to her growing fortune. Sometimes she was Ruth Tanner, Professional Geologist, and other times she was Susan Gardener Professional Thief. *Hell, she thought, life was strange.* She just wished she could remember her childhood before the coma.

She broke out of her deep reflections and noticed she had smoked another cigar while she had daydreamt. Ruth revved the Ski-Duo for a while, listening to the immense power. After letting it warm up, she headed out into the trail which was deeply covered. It had snowed hard for the last two days, not letting her get to her job site. She pointed the Summit HM Ski-Duo at the five foot high entrance and raced it up to the top.

Ruth paused for a moment at the top. She glances over the immense landscape, snow everywhere. It was covered with various types of Pine, Spruce and Birch trees. She could see that the rugged terrain was overlaid with about three to four feet of snow. Mountainous terrain could be seen to the north of the property. Ruth studied the terrain trying to remember where the trail should be. During the past two days the snow had totally covered up the trail. Virgin snow she thought, five miles of it before even getting to the line-cutters tent. There she planned to have a coffee and warm up before heading out to the baseline she was starting out from today.

She headed the ski-duo into the fresh powdered snow and it sank about a third into it. The snowmobiling was hard; it wanted to get stuck in the new soft snow. Two thirds forward the grid lines had been cut last year by strong local Aboriginal Indians and the rest was being finished off now. The deep virgin snow made her previous Bompas Property located on the east side of Elliot Lake like a kid's play yard. This property had steep hills, plenty of trees and lots water ways to cross over.

Ruth was good at handling a ski-duo, but she was finding herself getting increasingly hotter. She loosened her outfit. She wore a green hydro-line jacket with black ski pants underneath. On her hands were thick two fingered gloves designed to keep your hands warmer. On her head was a grey toque spotted with black and white designs. She loosened her black scarf tied around her neck so that it wouldn't fog up her ski-duo goggles. Completing her outfit was high waterproof with green boots with thick mustard colours soles. Inside her boots her feet were warm with a thick layer of blue felt and a pair of white socks and a pair of grey work socks. A person working alone in this country had to be ready for anything. *You can always take off the clothes according to the weather, but you can't add some safety provisions.* Strapped to the back of the Summit HM ski-duo was a large pair of snowshoes.

She noticed it at 10 AM, and decided to by pass the base-camp and go straight to ground zero. The property was cut like a giant plus sign. At the center of the grid it was know as 0+00. Lines were cut pedalled to the main east-west line run upwards to the north and down to the south. The same happened with lines being cut running parallel to the east and to the west. It was like a giant grid paper. All these lines help when readings were taken from her geophysical instrument inside her knapsack. At every hundred feet a stake was cut and jammed into the ground and a florescent tape marked with a black marker would indicate the location. When she took her geophysical reading she would mark down the location and the information into a small black note book with a pencil, later the information would be put down on to a map she was working on. Then she could decide from the readings if anything was going on underground that might indicate a geological formation that could be potentially interesting for test drill holes for further testing.

Her green hydro-line jacket was now soaked from sweat and dripping water falling off the trees. She parked the Summit HM ski-duo near the beginning of the property. As she stopped the ski-duo, she removed her green jacket draping it over the handle bars of the ski-duo. She jumped off the Summit HM ski-duo and sank three feet into the snow. *Virgin snow of course, what would she know about virgins being her age and still one.* She grabbed her snow shoes and strapped them on and pulled on her bath backpack. Her feet were warm in the high green rubber felt lined boots she wore. Very frustrating and harrowing start to the day and it was only 10:10 AM.

Changing her mind, she lifted her snowshoes above the snow line and snowshoe over to the group of line cutter's tents. She had a quick coffee with her hired help in one of their rough, yet large comfortable tents. After giving them a quick set of instructions, Ruth headed off down a freshly cut trail. She sank into the snow. Even with the snowshoes she was finding herself getting more soaked with each mile she walked. At the south end of the property she pulled out her EM-16 Unit and started doing Geophysical readings. The machine took the electric magnetic pulse at the location using frequencies from various stations located in Canada and the United States of America. The instrument looked like a six inch square box with a large handle on it. As she looked through the eye hole of the machine she tilted her body forward and backwards until the sound emitted from the box disappeared. Inside the eye hole she could see a circle with angles on it. Remembering the number, she wrote down the angle and the location it was taken at. Later that evening she would have fun translating it on to a paper map and then trying to make sense out of it.

After doing geophysical readings on several trail lines, she noticed a change in the weather. It was now starting to snow and the temperature was dropping quickly. She got to the end of a Cut-Line and couldn't find a Tie Line cutting across to Line 36 West. She noticed by her footprints that she had twice gone in a circle and somehow had come back to where she had started. She looked at the clouds and knew a change in weather was about to occur. She hurried back to her ski-duo only dressed in her black ski-pants, sweater, gloves and black toque. By the time she had arrived back at the ski-duo handles. She then smashed the ice off the jacket against a Birch tree and slipped into it. She had hoped to do another 2800 feet of geophysical readings, but the temperature was dropping too fast. Very soon it would be dark, so she headed the ski-duo back down the trail to the pickup truck. Ruth found it much earlier this time as the trail had been packed down by her morning travels.

She was starting to develop a bad headache and feared it would develop into a full fledged migraine. By the time she reached the pickup truck it was dark. Her gloves, jacket and the rest of her outfit were completely frozen. Her scarf had frozen with her frosty breath and mucus from her nose. She drove the Summit HM Ski-Duo up onto a small snow bank and backed the truck with the tailgate down into the snow bank. She then drove the ski-duo onto the back of the pickup. Ruth headed the pickup back to the warmth of the hotel.

She mentally compared this cold job with the extreme heat of her last job where she had worked for an Oil Discovery Project in Sandi Arabia. She decided she like the cold better than the heat, plus the fact that they didn't take kindly to strangers.

Finally, she arrived at the hotel and unpacked her gear located in the back of the pickup. From the corner of her left eye she thought she noticed a dark figure in the background shadows. She wondered if she was being followed. Coincident, she figured and pulled out a cigar. Ruth trimmed off a 1/4 inch off the end of the cigar with a small pair of scissors, studied the cigar, and felt good about cutting down on her smoking.

CHAPTER TWO

Elliot lake, Ontario, 10:00 PM, Friday Evening

Beyond the edge of the parking lot, a grey frosty mist swirled. The four intermingled with the dark moonless evening. Cold vapours clung low to the snow covered asphalt, twisting and twirling several upwards, covering the area leading up to the Bon Air Motel. Along the outskirts of the huge parking lot! In the darkness of the tree, Alyssa Lawless adjusted her large frame of a body into a more comfortable position. Alyssa shivered in the negative thirty-five degree Fahrenheit* temperature that surrounded her. The cold air didn't bother her. It was more of a sensation that affected her body. Alyssa was positive that she had finally tracked down her prey as she like to think of her.

Her tiny fist pushed aside a Spruce branch and pulled out a set of Raven Night Vision Binoculars. She had looked around at various types that the company produced but eventually decided on D212Pro version. They had oversized stereo lens that captured large amounts of light that was useful for surveillance work and just general observation. The binoculars were made of a light weight component that should withstand years of use. The D212Pro Raven Night Vision Binoculars were quite reasonably priced as to other night vision binoculars on the market, but Alyssa was tight with her money. *They better work for the price I paid for them, she thought.*

Manoeuvring herself out of the tightly packed trees, she edged her huge petty towards a huge snow bank. The pile of snow was continuously growing with the unusually large amount of snowfall that the season was producing. The huge snow plow trucks had pushed the snow to the edge of the parking lot. Later, large backhoes had lifted up the snow into a main pile at the corner edge of the property. Making sure as she moved out of the bush, that she remained hidden, she allowed the darkness, trees and mist to cast a dark shadow over her body. Alyssa then worked at pulling her immense body out of the deep snow and evergreens.

Alyssa was a tall woman. She stood around six feet, six inches tall and weighed over one hundred and fifty pounds of solid muscle. Her small rounded face was topped with a short dark brown pixie hair cut style. Alyssa only wore a colourful bandana. It was tied tightly around her forehead to keep the sweat from dripping down into her eyes. Being a tiny girl, she had a bad tendency to perspire constantly. Her friends nicknamed her shark and rarely called her Alyssa.

Rising up her muscular forearm, she lifted the Raven Night Vision Binoculars to her eyes and surveyed the layout of the Motel. The target detecting range was perfect so she then adjusted the vision knob on top for a clearer view. She could clearly see the top part of Ruth

Tanner through the corner unit window of the motel. *Strange* thought Alyssa, the *curtains were fully opened*. Ruth appeared to be working on a map and using a laptop computer as she shifted around the room.

She noticed that Ruth seemed anxious to complete the map of the property the she had worked on that day. Alyssa climbed up the large snow bank for a better viewing angle, watching closely, she saw Ruth's drafting tools move quickly as she plotted out the results of her day's geophysical activities. *Very anxious,* Alyssa thought. She watched as Ruth hurried to finish her drafting on the small foldout table that the Motel had provided for her work.

Next door, through the widely opened curtains, she could see people partying and drinking while listening to a deafening volume of music. She didn't need her binoculars to see that a wild party way underway. *Wonder why no one is complaining about the blaring music, she pondered.* Raising her D212 Pro Raven Night Vision Binoculars, she turned to examine the third unit from the end. Alyssa made a few adjustments on the binoculars. Climbing up higher to the top of the snow bank, she could just make out a line of vision to the third unit through the open curtains.

She watched as an old lady with a winter toque on her head sat down comfortably in front of a television. The machine emitted a soft green glowing light. Some type of nature channel program was playing. The old lady didn't seem to mind the party was going on next door. Since she wasn't complaining, it probably explained why the Motel management hadn't come knocking at her neighbours' door. *Usually after 9.PM, Motels required that music and loud noises be kept to a minimum for the guest's enjoyment and relaxation, Alyssa pondered.*

Alyssa returned her gaze back towards Ruth's unit at the end of the Motel. She was surprised as she watched Ruth getting dressed up into dark strapless dress complete with a matching black sweater with black silk padded shoulders. Amazed she pressed the binoculars close to her face with her tiny hands. Ruth was removing a pair of tinted small reading glasses and pulling off a make-believe wig. She scrubbed at her head with some hair gel and swirled it around. Her hair appeared to be dark brown. *What was going on, Alyssa wondered as she rubbed her eyes with her tiny hands.*

Ruth then placed a black eye patch over her right eye. She seemed to relax considerably after it covered her eye. Ruth bent over stuffing things into some type of bag material. Alyssa's position didn't allow her to see what was happening on the Motel floor.

Ruth then moved out of Alyssa's sight of vision. All she could see were lights flickering as a television set was turned on. A pair of green boots propped themselves onto the top edge of a chair. Although she couldn't see Ruth, she figured she must be relaxing and adjusting herself into a more comfortable position. The lights dimmed lower. *Ruth must be setting down to watch some relaxing television show, Alyssa thought.* Another wasted night. Not much happening here. She looked over at the room next door, the crowd inside was raising an uproar of music, laughter and shouting. They appeared to be enjoying a Friday evening.

The door to the furthest unit opened. Out walking the old lady dressed in a green ski suit with yellow patches on it. Grey stringy long dirty hair peaked out of a green toque with large white pom-pom on top. She had it pulled down hard on her head against the bitter cold. The old lady didn't appear to be very tall, nor did she seem to be in very good shape. Around her waist, she seemed to be packing a few to many beer muscles.

Alyssa glanced back at Ruth's place where the lights had turned back on. She could only see Ruth's boot rocking back and forth. At the same time, she could see the TV channels changing from one to the other as Ruth tried to find an interesting program to watch. All she could see of Ruth was her work boots shifting restlessly.

The old lady took out a pipe and stuffed some tobacco into it. She then proceeded to lit it with a cigar lighter. Although! The old lady seemed to exude confidence. She scrutinized the area around the parking lot as she put the lighter back to the pipe, getting a fresh puff of smoke coming from her pipe. *Was she surveying her environment, Alyssa wondered?*

The old lady noticed people near the street approaching the Motel. Dropping her pipe behind her back, the old lady began stumbling drunkenly towards the main street. Mumbling and cursing to herself, she almost tripped and roughly shoved her way through the group of people. She staggered out of the parking lot and turned right onto the Main Street.

Got you, you clever little bastard, thought Alyssa. She was convinced that Ruth had pulled a switch identity. Possibly in-case she was wrong, she walked up to the

Ruth's end unit and looked in the window. Her jaw dropped and she as stunned at what she saw in the room.

Quickly, Alyssa strolled towards the main street and followed in the direction that Ruth had gone. She barely missed her as she turned a street corner and headed in a new direction. No longer was Ruth stumbling and appearing to be inebriated.

Following from a distance it dawned on her, why it had taken her so long to find her. Ruth switched characters and could manipulate her environment to throw off anyone from finding her. *Why though, she's an owner of a large legitimate Geological Exploration Company.* She seems to be an actress, with some type of reason for her behaviour. A ghost and an enigma all rolled up together. Alyssa as following a phantom that changed like the mist swirling around her feet.

Alyssa with her small rounded face, petty body and swaggering like walk was no dummy. She had studied and excelled at chemistry at university. She had easily obtained a higher than average grade point than her peers. Alyssa enjoyed parties, beer, men and plenty of food to eat; she never had to study hard. Learning chemistry came easy to her. Her father had been a Chemical Engineer and had started teaching her chemistry from a very early age. By the time she was twelve years old, she knew more about chemistry than most adults. At school, she was a constant challenge to her teacher.

During her spare time she hung out at the gyms doing heavy free weights with the locals. She constantly pushed herself to do that extra few pounds to her routine. Also, Alyssa loved the sport of boxing. She was good at it and moved lightly for her size. Her friends joked that whatever shark hit went down for the count.

Ruth's mind was on her acting and didn't notice that she was being followed. She turned another corner and headed up a long deserted street. Thru trees were snow covered. Branches hung low at a curved angle from the weight of the snow. It looked like a tunnel in the darkness. As she reached the top of the hill, Ruth turned left onto a barely plowed driveway. She entered the brushes near the driveway and disappeared.

As Alyssa approached the driveway, she peered down a curving lane way. Looking upwards, she noticed a large house set high up on a hill top with an immense wall encircling it. The house was huge and appeared to be made of large grey granite carved blocks. It had very few windows featured on the side of the mansion. Two large spires, about thirty feet apart reached up towards the sky. They looked like fangs of a giant bat. *Spooky, she thought, glad she wasn't going to be visiting what looked like the house from hell.* Entering the bushes across the street, she settled down for what could be a long wait.

CHAPTER THREE

Elliot Lake, Ontario, 10:15 PM, Friday Evening

Ruth Tanner prepared to exit from her corner unit of the Bon Air Motel using the interconnecting doors between the Motel rooms. She had rented them out under assumed names. Tonight she wanted to give the impression that she was still in her room.

Using plug-in timers to alter the impression of lights, she modified the illumination to give different variation of friction. A miniature motor, linked to a rocking chair, pulled down the end of the rocking chair and then returned it to its previous position. *Attached on top, with their fishing line, were green knee length boots that she had used that day out in the brush.* A pair of jeans filled with material, swayed to the motion of the moving chair. The rocking chair was connected to the bed with a couple of bungee cords. Ruth wanted to give the impression that she was relaxing, moving comfortably on another chair. She had programmed the television to change channels every few minutes. Anyone doing surveillance on her unit would most likely believe that she was still in her room relaxing.

She lifted up her padded hockey duffel bag in the flickering light. It contained only a light black knapsack with a pillow on each side. It looked like a heavy bag carried by a hockey player. From the corner of the room she grabbed a battered up beige hockey stick. Turning it over she felt the rough tape tied tightly around the curved edge. It was well used and perfect for her evening plans.

Ruth Tanner clothing consisted of a black sweater with dark shiny silk shirt with shoulder pads and black pants with large pockets on the sides. She wore a black wool toque on her head while a black eye patch filled comfortably over her right eye. Finishing off her outfit was a pair of black military boots, a black fabric like belt, and on her hands she wore a pair of tight black leather gloves.

She knocked hard three times on the interconnecting door which joined up to the next room. A young lady holding a beer bottle in her hand opened up the door. A cigarette hung loosely out of her mouth. Wild music blared out of the room. Inside were about fifteen people drinking and dancing. Disgustedly, she looked at the mess in the room. It was a terrible sight. Pizza boxes, beer bottles and full ashtrays littered the tables and chairs in the room. Some were dancing, others listening to music while gulping down the free beer she had purchased for their use. Some of the couples were starting to get to intimate on the double beds.

They were all too drunk to take her seriously in her outfit. Ruth looked at the young lady who had opened the door. She was dressed in jeans with a white work shirt. Her dirty blond hair was sticking up, probably

24

with the use of hair gel. *Glancing up at her, Ruth handed her a roll of money and said "Make it look like the party is winding down, clean up this room and start leaving in an hour. I don't want the maid cleaning up this shit-hole in the morning. I've paid you and your friends a lot of money tonight, keep it to yourselves or I may hear about it. Believe it or not, you don't want to hear back from me."* Ruth grabbed a girl and her boy partner by their elbows, lifted them off their feet, and used those shields as she walked across the room.

She knocked twice, waited and knocked twice again on the door to the next unit. It connected this Motel unit to the second unit from her room. The door slowly opened by an old woman. Inside the room, it was dark except for a television playing a late night television show. "At least your room is clean compared to that dump next door." The old women nodded. "I may be a bum used to sleeping in the streets but I appreciate that you've let me have a roof over my head and food to eat. Nobody has ever done that for me. Thank you."

Ruth nodded, probably the closest she ever came to saying you're welcome. She had found the women sleeping outdoors in an alleyway one evening and offered to bring her in for a coffee. After a coffee, Ruth had a conversation with her over a warm meal. She had learned that the old women used to work in one of the local mines. The mine had closed and she was laid off from her job. Her husband then filed for a divorce. Later, after looking for work she found that her husband had cleared out the small house that they had lived in for five years. He had then proceeded to clean out all of their money in their joint account from the bank. She couldn't pay for her mortgage and the bank foreclose on her taking away her house.

She was devastated. The old women had no place to go. After asking for help from her friends, she soon discovered what friendship was, when none was offered. Depression set in. Soon she as forced to sleep on the street in a cardboard box for protection against the wind. She had no family, no friends and nothing to look forward to. Until that one night when Ruth had discovered her huddled and shivering, almost frozen stiff in the blistering cold.

Ruth offered her the room with a restaurant tab in exchange for some work that she needed done. She looked over at the old women and said "*Nice toque.*" The old women nodded slyly and said "*It keeps the cold off my head, eh. Over on the bed is everything that you asked for, I'll stay over here like you told me and keep away from the window.*"

Ruth started putting on a colourful green and yellow ski suit with green ski pants over her outfit. She then slipped a fake wig on top of her head. The old women passed her, her toque and slipped it over the fake wig on her head. Ruth then shoved her eye patch up under the toque. Looking in the mirror at herself and turning around she asked the old women to pass her a pillow. She stuffed it under her ski-suit. Now with a pair of fake glasses and a pipe in her mouth she looked different.

"Thanks Tammy, you're good women. You can have this room until the end of the winter, along with a restaurant account. I'm wanted to offer you a job position in my company. Not out of pity or because you need it, but because you're a good women, and you know the area and the mining around it. I need a woman that I can trust to manage my properties in the area. Later, I'll offer you another geology related position that will bring you back into a better life that you deserve." The old women had tears flowing down her face. No one, not one person she had known in the last five years of living and working in the area had offered to help her in her time of need, except this one woman and who she didn't even know. *"Thank you. I feel like a real woman again because of you. Ruth, after all that you've done for me, you can trust that I'll work hard for you."* Ruth looked her in her eyes and then shook her hand. Open the door Ruth entered out into the dark, the freezing cold weather.

CHAPTER FOUR

Elliot Lake, Ontario, 10:25 PM, Friday Evening

The change in appearance was astonishing. Ruth Tanner or Susan Gardener as she now was known was dressed in a black dress suit underneath. On the outside she sported a bright green ski suit, matching pants and a green toque with a bright Pom Pom on top. Susan stepped outside of Motel unit number 113 and carried the large hockey bag in one hand and grabbed the hockey stick in the other. Leaning against the wall, she stopped to smoke her pipe at the same time being careful not to burn her fake skin or hair sticking out from her toque. She checked out the area for anything out of the ordinary. The shadows around the parking lot were quite dark, she noticed and very foggy. She usually had feelings about something being wrong, but she couldn't spot anything out of the ordinary. Nothing tonight seemed different.

Nothing, just a group of people walking up the driveway, Ruth or Susan as she was now known dropped her pipe behind her and started walking unsteadily, wobbling as if drunk. Leaning heavily on her hockey stick, she mumbled to herself as she past by the group of people. She wanted the people to pay attention to her and the way she dressed. The ski suit was coming off later for good. If anything went wrong tonight all the people would remember was a colourful and mumbling drunk walking the streets of Elliot Lake.

During the past three weeks she had been eyeing a grey stone building rising up high on the hill top. It sat lonely in a patch of evergreens. The high stone walls had a dark forbidding look. The mansion had two green peaked towers located at each end of the roof. Weather vanes were located on tops of each of the peaked towers.

She walked down a few roads and then turned down a dark, depressing Side Street. After walking down the snow covered tunnel-like road Susan entered a slippery driveway. Slipping into a bushy patch of trees she removed her ski suit. She was now attired in her black pants and a black sweater. She pulled off her colourful toque. She then removed her fake skin and hair piece showing the black toque below. Susan pulled down her black eye patch over her right eye and felt the comfort it gave her as it settled into place.

Hanging from her belt was her weapon of choice, her leather club with the oval bronzita ball entwined in leather. Susan tightened her pair of leather gloves and removed the black knapsack from the hockey duffel bag. She swung it over her two shoulders, and attached a Velcro strap around her waist to hold the Knapsack firmly. Susan then put her ski suit and the rest of her costume into the hockey bag and shoved it in the heavy bushes around the solid grey wall.

Susan started climbing up the ten foot wall as quick as a cat. She flipping over the wall, using a move she practiced previously. She landed on the far side of the bushy garden area. *It was filled with miniature ponds and bridges and looked quite nice in the moonlight, she thought.* Glancing around with her good right eye, she twisted her head to take in the surroundings.

Susan discovered more than the average security system. Something was definitively weird about this place. All the windows and doors were heavily protected with security systems. Quickly, she removed her whip like handle with its brown heavily wore leather covering with the braided oval bronzita ball. She had studied the oval bronzita ball continuously over the past few years. All she could make of it was that it had a pattern similar to the continents on the earth. It appeared to have a dark ruby jewel located near the top that even she couldn't recognize.

She flicked the club shaped handle and the oval bronzita ball whipped up the wall tying it's self around a cement object. She climbed the six feet and repeated the process several times. Each time she luckily managed to find a rock like outcrop. No more whip now she decided, and climbed the last several feet to the top of the green pointed roof. A skylight was located on two sides of the green spire life roof.

Susan reached back into her black knapsack and removed a sixty foot knotted rope with three sharp hooks on the end. She then removed a large glass cutter and suction cup. Susan licked the suction cup. Faking a disgusted look, she stuck it to the glass. After that she attached the glass cutter to the center of the suction cup. Susan gave it a few turns around and felt the glass loosening. She tugged the suction cup, which snapped the glass from the other glass around it. Susan quickly unhooked the glass from the suction cup and placed it on a flat area of the roof.

Attaching the grapple end of the hook to the nearest secure location she could find, she dropped the rope into the darkness below. Susan slipped her feet. Then her body through the round opening, careful not to cut herself on its sharp edges. She then started to climb down the knotted rope. It was about a thirty foot drop to the floor, she estimated as each knot was one foot apart. Silence and complete darkness was that entire she could see as she strained her one good eye to adjust to the room's lighting.

She felt a surface under her left legs, but none under her right leg. She started to lose her balance and strained to remain upright in the darkness. Had she land on a part of the wall, a staircase or possibly the edge of a deep hole? Susan felt a sudden fear as she strained to find the rope in the darkness and grab it before she dropped over the edge.

CHAPTER FIVE

Elliot Lake, 11:00 PM
Friday Evening

Littleone Whitefeater, aboriginal Indian, was crouched on the floor with her legs crossed tightly together. Her arms were folded inward, with the thumbs of her fist pushing tightly against her massive chest. Her eyes were closed, but her head remained pointed forward. Each evening she meditated deep in thought. Often she crossed the barrier between conscious thought and an area where she was free of all distractions. Here she could roam around thinking clearly. When in this zone of thought, her mind was free to focus on any subject.

Tonight she was bothered with troubled thoughts. Something was wrong she thought to herself. She had slipped into the barrier and it forecasted trouble. There was something indistinguishable. Littleone Whitefeater, deep in meditation with her thoughts, couldn't predict what problems were about to arise.

Opening her eyes, she woke herself up from her trance. Stretching backwards, loosening up her stiff muscles. She realized that something was about to occur.

Standing up she looked into a mirror on the wall. Littleone shook her long black shoulder length hair and rubbed her face with her small hands. She could see a rugged, dark complexion with a nose proportioned like a crow. Since her youth, she had grown into a petty women standing five feet, ten inches and weighted around one hundred and twenty pounds. Her large muscular shoulders and biceps strained against the expensive white dress shirt that she wore. Examining herself in the floor to ceiling mirror, she took off her white shirt and grey dress pants. She stood clad only in aboriginal Indian leather shorts. They were made with smooth buckskin and decorated around the waist with a belt of ornamental Indians beads. The front and back hung down above her muscular tights while it left the sides open for easy movement.

Around her wrists she wore decorated wrist bands. Tied tightly around her huge biceps were leather straps. Littleone was proud of her shaped and worked hard at keeping it looking like a professional body builder. Thoughts about not knowing future problems brought on a terrible anger. She raised her arms as if posing for a body building contest. Littleone then pumped up her upper limbs until the leather tied around her biceps strained against it. Both leather decorations snapped off at the same time.

Littleone, her adopted mother had given her that name. She had given this name since a young age. Littleone had never told her anything about her past or even what her real name was. Vaguely, she remembered living at an orphanage before that age.

*   *   *

She had been about ten years old when she was adopted along with thirteen other young children by a grisly qualities of the innocent looking, tall, thin woman who seemed nice enough. Oddly, the lady dressed in only one colour. Littleone remember clearly how dashing the women had looked in her expensive purple velvet buttoned suit jacket and matching slacks. Her shirt was a slightly lighter shade of purple while she carefully made up tie matched her dress clothes. Walking into the orphanage with her shiny purple leather shoes, the woman had tightly gripped a purple walking stick with a huge Amethyst jewel on top.

Littleone and her blond scruffy friend had watched through the tinted glass as the lady had tipped her purple fedora hat to the Matron of the orphanage. Clearly they saw how she had charmed the gentleman. Reaching down her hand with a smoky amethyst jewel on a pewter ring, she took his hand and barely kissed it. Her hypnotic eyes held his attention; it seemed that he was held captive by those eyes. Waving her hands in the air, she expressed something that the girls couldn't hear. Pulling out a large roll of money tightly wrapped with a rubber band from under her hat, she watched as his greedily eyes stared at it. Smoothly she whispered in his ear. A shocked look came into his eyes, but then they wandered back to examine the huge roll of money.

An arrangement was made that night. In exchange for the money, the lady was allowed to select fourteen girls from the orphanage. The plans she had the girls were to be kept secret. Over the next few weeks, she wined and dined the Matron. Taking her time she studied the young girls at the orphanage. She observed them and studied their flies. Slowly, she began to decide on which orphans she planned on adopting. Littleone and Carrie were the first two she decided on. She saw exactly what she was looking for in them. Their names and identities were to be changed. She renamed Littleone because of the shape of her nose and the colour of her hair.

Along with her was her friend, a scraggly, dirty hair youth. The Female Suffrage had nicknamed her Carrie, because she said that her mother had once been in a horror movie by trade. Later, when she couldn't afford to keep the youth, she had her placed in the orphanage.

Seemingly, the lady was choosing kids that were tough and had lived a hard life. Ten more kids were carefully chosen. She was not in a rush. Wandering around the school yard, she had watched as two teams of six players played a rough game of football against each other. One team seemed wilder, yet friendlier towards each other. They wore muddy jeans and ripped-up tee-shirts. An impressive sized kid with a light shade of brown hair brought her friends together in a huddle. Obviously they were discussing their next play. The lady recognized that the kid was the Quarterback of the team. Preparing to throw the football, she looked both ways as her five other friends assumed their positions. She passed back the ball, carefully watching as her friends ripped into the other team. Running quickly but with amazing agility a small but fast young teammate ran quickly by the offence. She caught the ball as it thrown like a bullet to her. The lady was astonished at the speed and agility of the youth as she ran for the touchdown.

She had simply pointed her finger at the large youth and the smaller girl as their friends watched. When it came time to leaving there were problems with this group of six kids. They had always been friends always at the orphanage. The group of friends didn't want to be broken up. The lady insisted and she was not one to be turned down. The six friends were broken up as a group but they swore to stay in contact. The Matron and the lady erased all of the records of the fourteen children. It was as they had never existed.

The purple clad lady tipped her fancy hat to him and handed him the huge roll of money. She asked him to count it in a safe place where no one would find notice. Later that evening he tugged of the elastic band and unrolled the money. He started playing with it in his hand. *Money; lots of money; he thought, just to get rid of those brats.* The matron stacked up the money and started counting the bills. Frequently, as his fingers dried, he licked his fingers to moisten the paper currency making it easier to count.

The matron gasped. He couldn't breath. He could feel himself becoming paralyzed and turning a deep shade of red. Slowly turning his head, he watched as the lady opened the door, and sat down in front of him. She was watching him die and enjoying it. As he died, she reached down for the poisoned money and rubber band with a set of tight purple doe skin leather gloves. She rolled up the money and put on the rubber band and put it in her pocket. From another pocket, she removed a jar of the poison and placed it on the table along with a typed letter which she crumpled and placed carefully in one of his hands. She placed the poison jar partially emptied in his other hand.

She stood up, looking around, and thought out every idea that the police could think of. It was perfect in every detail; a lonely man dating a dashing womanan had committed suicide when she left. No clues as to her identity or where she was. These type of things happened everyday. Certainly a suicide the police would probably assume. The lady closed the door.

Rounding up the kids, she placed them in a large van. Overtime, the fourteen children were brought up into Northern Canada. It was freezing cold land full of barren landscape, icy glaciers, frozen snow and rugged mountains. This was Baffin Island, a frozen wasteland located near the Arctic Circle. Eventually they arrived at a rough old log cabin designated the Female Suffrage's Cabin in a Park Reserve called Baffin Island Park. From that day forward, Littleone came to call the lady, the Female Suffrage.

* * *

Littleone office, where she preferred to do her business and meditations was uniquely decorated. Weapons of her culture, tomahawks, spears, knifes and different bows and arrows proudly hung on the walls. Mounted against the rich dark wood of the walls were stuffed heads of bear, moose, mountain lion, deer and other wild animals. Photos of famous aboriginal Indians from Canada were creatively framed along with relics that they had possessed in their past lives. The rustic hand made frames perfectly matched her office decor.

She walked barefooted on a thick light brown carpet over to her huge solid desk. It was created from a slab of a large tree from British Columbia and made into a desk. A medium stain and varnish allowed the center rings of the tree's growth pattern to easily be studied. Behind her desk was a large black padded leather chair on wheels, resting on a hard brown ceramic floor area.

Walking over to a classy rolling bar, with a built in fridge, she gazed appreciatively at a set of antique crystal glasses and matching crystal decanter. The decanter was filled with a very old and hard to obtain brandy. Littleone poured herself a still amount of the aged alcohol and sniffed at it. Smelling carefully, she appreciated the heady and fine aroma that exuded from large bowl shaped brandy glass. Feeling a bit of a chill, she put back on her expensive Black dress pants and white stiff necked blouse. She then added a black snake skin belt and black dress shoes. She splashed on lightly very expensive perfume. Finally, she added under her blouse collar a bolo-tie, made with braided dark leather with a large bear claw and feathers hanging down between her open blouse fronts. On the end of the bolo-tie leather ties were small wolverine claws.

She figured on picking up a couple of Native men and bringing them to her apartment in town. She brought no one to her large mansion. It was all business at this location.

Littleone open up a sealed humidor and removed an expensive cigar kept at the correct temperature and

JESSICA YELLOWKNIFE

humidity. Picking up her crystal brandy stiffer glass, she walked over to a crackling large fireplace with its metal screen door in front. Drinking slowly, she lit the handmade cigar custom make to her preference. She inhaled the fine cigar and sipped at the aged brandy gazing deeply into the simmering, fireplace.

* * *

Lately, she had been thinking of her past. Months had been spent on Baffin Island. Later, she had been dropped off by her adopted mother, whom she knew only, as the Female Suffrage at a Private School in Ottawa, Ontario. She had been given special instructions that she was to learn or she would be beaten severely with a cane. *Good incentive, thought Littleone.* Along with her on the trip was the scraggy, dirty haired youth nicknamed Carrie.

* * *

Littleone and Carrie were eventually made Captains in the Female Suffrage grand scheme they knew their part of the operation, and had decided that she had similar operations in other countries. They answered only to her. Her other adopted children answered only to Littleone and Carrie. They had seven captains working for them. Each of these captains had recruited two ladies to work for them. After that each of these ladies became captains, and recruited another two ladies to work for them.

From here each new group of two ladies working together continued to recruit two new ladies. This pattern of recruiting had continued on since 1980 this had gone one until a shape of a pyramid had formed with around 120 members working in Canada. From Canada the secret recruiting program had continued on throughout the United States of America, then into Central America, the Caribbean Islands and slowly developing into South America. There was no shortage of ladies and men who were impressed by the plan and wanted in. Each partner knew the other and worked together. They took instructions from their immediate senior who had taken them under her wings.

The interesting thing about this operation was that partners never knew any of the members above their boss. If they had problems they went to their recruiter, who answered to her superior. She either gave them instructions or asked her boss. Mainly, it was handled immediately. Very rarely did it have to go up the chain of command to Littleone and Carrie, but if problems or questions occurred, it went directly to the Female Suffrage.

Questions went up the chain of command and directions came down the chain of command. In this way, if the Police broke a link in the chain of the operation, the individual members didn't have any knowledge of the different members.

As far as Littleone and Carrie knew they controlled somewhere over 2000 ladies in North America, Central America, the Caribbean's and South America. The pyramid roughly formed about seven levels. The Female Suffrage who controlled the operations formed the seventh and highest level of command. The second level was operated by Littleone and Carrie, and each was given a unique peridot ball with an embedded Rudy jewel as their symbol of authority. The next three levels below, with the seven other ladies who had been adopted from the orphanage, were referred to as the moonstones level. They were called the organizers. Each was given a ball made of pure silver of moonstone with the unique Sapphire jewel embedded into it. The next two levels below were referred as the glass poppy jasper levels. They assisted the organizers in making sure that the operation went according to plan. Each member was given a glass poppy jasper ball with a unique oval bronzita jewel. The balls were a present from the Female Suffrage and symbolized their part in the Pyramid.

The next three levels in the pyramid were always chosen carefully for their skills, social position or connections. They were known as the specialists, and they were the ones who carried out the Female Suffrages plans. No symbol was given to them, being known as a specialist with honours enough. These last three levels operated from the top of Canada to the tip of South America.

It was a well planned operation, cleverly designed by the Female Suffrage. She had sat in her special chair, controlling crime and terror in Canada since 1970 watching it slowly develop. Slowly, near the end of the Century, the Female Suffrage had expanded her operations outside of Canada.

* * *

Littleone stared through her crystal glass into the fire and thought further how clever the Female Suffrage was. She had set up each Littleone and Carrie as partners each *working* together to control an empire. If there was a problem anywhere, they went for instructions to their leader.

Littleone refilled her brandy glass once more and lit up another cigar. She sat down behind her desk on the leather chair and propped up her legs on the tree table. Slowly, with the help of the brandy, she thought how utterly clever the Female Suffrage was. She had foreseen how terror could be brought to the World. The third level, the organizers, each with a moonstone ball with onyx embedded jewel under the command of Littleone and Carrie, the Female Suffrage had made each captain an organizer of a specialty criminal activity. The seven young ladies at the top of the pyramid were organizers. Safety, they hid their silver moonstone embedded balls, gifts from the Female Suffrage.

The Female Suffrage had thought deeply and foreseen the future of terror and made her organizers control a special area. One Captain of Asian based organized crimes. Another was in charge of controlling the East European based Organized Crime syndicates. The Female Suffrage had placed the third Captain at Marine Ports, Airports and Land Crossings and in charge of organized Unions. The fourth Captain controlled the various Motorcycle gangs across the counties. The fifth Captain controlled the traditional aboriginal based families while the six Captains controlled the Aboriginal Indians based organized crime throughout the different countries. The seventh Captain controlled the youth through Street Gangs across the vast area, technology, and sexual exploitation of children and the illicit movement of Firearms.

Three of them were tossed in as wild cards, each with a bronze ball with an embedded oval bronzita jewel, to watch over the activities of all the operatives. They reported separately to the Female Suffrage, no one, not even Littleone or Carrie knew who they were. They were considered spies in the organization, in case people started to take matters into their own hands. They had their own people assisting them. Littleone and Carrie often wondered who they were and if they knew them.

*   *   *

As perfect as any plan could be. Except that Littleone had to be given another golden Peridot ball. She had been lost when at a young age she had knocked unconscious one of the original group that escaped back in 1980. She had hit the youth hard on the side of her head and used the golden Peridot ball to gauge out the youth's right eye. Littleone had assumed that she had killed her. Stupidly, she had dropped her precious symbol next to her victim and forgot about it until later. The Female Suffrage upon hearing that she was still alive had her framed and locked up in jail for the rest of her life. Littleone didn't feel like dwelling on that now. It always made her upset. The Female Suffrage had been angry with her and had beaten her severely. Later, she might think about it, but not now.

The Female Suffrage wasn't perfect. She had made a mistake also by letting two of the fourteen children escape. Long ago on that evening, when all the children that the Female Suffrage had assembled at her cabin on Auyuittuq National Park Reserve on Baffin Island back in 1980. The two damn kids had been fast and clever and upon hearing of the Female Suffrage's plan had quickly disappeared. Littleone heard years later that the puny youth had been let out of jail. All attempts by the Female Suffrage to find her had failed. Littleone often wondered what had become of those kids who knew of their plans. She mediated again, thinking deeply, crossed over into the outer limits of conscious thought and deep meditative darkness.

CHAPTER SIX

Elliot Lake, 11:15 PM
Friday Evening

Susan perched precariously on her left leg while feeling emptiness below her other leg. In the dark it was an effort to maintain her balance. She felt like she was standing on the edge of an abyss. Susan felt helpless as she tried to retrieve the rope in the darkness. Concentrating and focusing her mind, she felt her balance returning to her. She reached into her side pocket for mini yet powerful flashlight. Feeling a knob on the side of the flashlight she gave it a few cranks forward. Susan then turned it on.

Susan looked around with her left eye. She had lowered herself down onto a huge pool table. Saw that she was perched on the edge of the huge pool table with only a four foot drop to a hardwood floor. Looking upwards, she could see her rope still swinging from the glass archway, where she had lowered herself.

Reaching down lightly with the palm of her hand on the edge of the pool table, Susan silently landed on a wooden floor. The hardwood oak floor was clean yet well used. Not a sound could be heard as her feet landed quietly on the oak floor. Susan moved catlike, No noise was made which might betray her presence to someone in the mansion. Susan turned off her flashlight as she reached into her knapsack for a single lenses night vision goggle. She strapped the single lenses over her good eye onto her forehead. A little adjusting and it fit comfortably over her left eye. It had a battery until built into it. Switching it on she could now see clearly through a green dim light of which no one else could see.

Looking at the wall, she was amazed to see a large map of the Elliot Lake and the surrounding districts. The detail was amazing. It showed all the local properties not currently in operation and those presently being worked on. Latitude and longitude ran both ways on the map. Susan still dumbfounded, examined the map closely and found that it was around thirty feet long and about six feet high.

The map was the one of the most detailed geological maps that she had ever seen. In great detail, the map was moulded with moulding paste to depict the terrain and hand painted to show the rivers, lakes, forests and valleys. It even showed where the beaver dams were located. Susan looked closely and studied the different properties currently under study. Some were using geological exploration techniques such as geophysics, geochemistry and drill whole operations to obtain core samples. It covered a large area from Swastika to Elliot Lake to King Elliot to Larder Lake, Quebec. Each town was roughly about 10 miles apart.

Walking over to another side wall she found a highly detailed map of Canada. Following the corner, she came to a large map of the USA. On the wall she found a rack of the most excellent pool cue sticks that she had ever seen. On the rack was a large blackboard, chalk and most peculiarly round leather paper weights. *No windows or doors she noted.* Glancing upwards at the large ceiling, she could see her rope leading upwards into the darkness towards the unseen high peaked gables. She took off her night goggles and switched on her small black flashlight.

The flashlight in itself was interesting in that it didn't need batteries. She cranked the knob on the side until it stopped and then adjusted the end of the flashlight to full glare. It could be turned the other way to make an almost laser like fineness of illumination. On the front in two small metal cases were spare light bulbs. The flashlight was waterproof and very strong.

Waking up from her thoughts, she walked over to the next wall and unexpectedly found a detailed map of the world. Strangely, near the edge of the map was a framed oil painting of Queen Victoria in her youth. Bizarre thought Susan, an entertainment room and a map room together. The only furnishings were the pool table, the framed painting, four chairs in the corners and the pool rack.

The Entertainment room was a mask. Why else would the leather paper weights are there, except for holding down the corners of the large maps spread out on the pool table?

Walking over to the large map of the Elliot Lake area she examined the map close up. She knew the properties the around the area pretty well. She had spent the last month doing geological exploration work on three separate properties that she owned the mineral rights to.

She let her hand glide over the latitude and longitude lines. Susan could feel that there was a crease running between the lines going in both directions. Reaching for the bottom latitude of the property that she was working on she gave it a pull. Smoothly it rolled outwards. Along the edge of the cabinet was attached a plastic sleeve with a roller which allowed it to glide out with ease. Inside was a long narrow box with twelve tubes filled with rolled up maps. Susan grabbed each of the maps, used the paper weights on the corners and laid them out on the pool table. Upon close examination she noticed that these were maps of the property she was currently working on. *These maps have finer detail on them than anything she was presently drafting up, she thought.*

Since it was her property she was working on, she opened up her knapsack and carefully folded up the maps and slipped them into her knapsack. A small sheet of paper fell out from amongst the maps. Taking a quick look at it she suddenly swore under her breath. They knew every secret detail about the property down to the fact that she had discovered a Kimberlitic Pipe. This was a geological underground structure which might indicate the presence of diamonds on her property. Not a new thing in Ontario, Diamond mining might soon be replacing the depleting gold mines in the area. As far as she knew it was a secret. She couldn't figure out how anyone else could have found out about it.

She soon discovered that each of the four walls had hidden drawers with maps and reports hidden within.

She walked over to map of Northern Ontario had found the closest latitude and longitude to her property. Susan pulled out the sliding door and placed all of the maps inside her knapsack. My property! Hell with them. She decided as she walked over to the framed picture of Queen Elizabeth in her youth. Really fits into this room. She reflected as she bowed before the picture. First she tried the left side to see if it would open but it didn't. Then she tried the right side and it effortlessly opened. It was held in place by tiny magnets on the frame which stuck to small metal places located behind the picture. She had assumed a safe would be located behind it, and was correct. Susan had figured it to be something more modern. It looked too easy, so she fought the urge to open it up immediately.

Feeling like a mouse in a cage! She looked around and figured she could always climb out the way she had come in, but Susan always like to have an alternative escape route. No door in the room she wondered, yet this were obviously an actively used room. She tried pulling on the pool cues, but no amount of pulling was moving that heavy display unit. She cranked her flashlight and reset it to full beam. Dropping to her knees, she examined the floor in front of the pool rack for a clue as to how the people came into the map room. The floor had a slight layering of dust on it. She picked up a few pieces up a few of dried ground made from people walking on it. She then noticed a footprint. It was huge, and must have been made from some large and heavy person. Looking closer, she noticed that the dust was showing a 90 degree arc from the pool rack attached to the wall.

Leaping to her feet, she pulled at the pool rack where the arc started and a large doorway swung open. It was dusty on the edges, but she noticed that above her good eye that the dust was smoothly cleaned away on both side. This doorway was bigger than an average doorway but the person who came in had clearly swiped her shoulders on both sides of the entrance. Susan concluded that this woman stood around six feet tall had big shoulders and was probably very heavy with big feet. Yeah, she's a monster alright, probably related to Frankenstein. Looking up the entrance she saw a cement block staircase with no rails, but with lights set into the walls near the bottom of each step.

Leaving the doorway opened, she moved towards the safe. As she approached it, Susan removed a pair of stethoscopes from her knapsack and put them in her ears. She then put the suction end up against the turning knob of the safe. This was child's play for one such as herself. She put the knapsack onto the floor and opened it up. As she swung open the safe! An alarm rang out! Just, as she had feared. Moving fast she scooped the contents of the safe into her opened knapsack. Later she could examine what she had removed. Amazement stopped her in her tracks as noticed a round gold Peridot ball at the back of the safe. Reaching in, she pulled it out and held it in her hands. She couldn't help but notice that it was the exact duplicate gold Peridot ball as the one she used as a weapon. It even has that strange colourful jewel on it with continents of the earth engraved around it.

A burst of noise could be heard upstairs as several people rushed through the home. A fumbling noise could be heard at the doorway located at the top of the stairs, as someone tried several keys rushing to find the correct one. *Time to get out of here, she concluded.* She leaped to the top of the pool table in one smooth move and grabbed the rope. She climbed as quickly as she could to the ceiling, and then carefully tried to exit out through the round hole in the glass that she had removed. She pulled up the rope just before the people entered the map door. As she stood on the roof top, stuffing the rope into her knapsack, the glass cracked sending a fine shower of glass silver downward onto the pool table. *Damn, Susan thought, always something.*

Moving like a spider, she climbed down the outside wall and landed softly in the garden. A door burst open and out poured four aboriginal Indians. *They were big and tough looking, Susan thought.* At the moment they couldn't located her, but she could clearly see them with her night goggle. Glancing around! She searches for a way out of the garden and up the ten foot wall.

Susan moved her stepped on the dry branch. All of them turned towards the cracking noise. As one they all leapt towards her at once. Side stepping! She brought her hand swiftly downward with her thumb pushed tightly against her folded fingers. She didn't make a fist but used her hand like a sword as she brought it down hard on the back of the person's neck. In the dark someone punched her hard in her stomach, causing her to fold over slightly while the person threw an upper cut to her chin. She played possum for a second. Catching them off guard, she swung a round house punch followed by a front kick at her opponent.

Dropping to her knees, she crossed her right leg over her left foot, turned around quickly, and kicked backwards delivering a powerful back kick to the person's abdomen. Susan felt good as she heard a terrible smothering of noise as her opponent tried to catch her breath. The other two had grabbed her by her forearms. *Wrong move, she thought as they all stove to push her towards.* Quickly, using their arms she pushed against the wall and executed a front flip which released her from their powerful grip. Turning around, she grabbed each of them by their necks, and pushed with her legs as hard as she could driving their heads into the granite wall.

No more fun, she thought. She turned and ran towards the wall, leaping up onto the back of the woman kneeling in pain on the ground. Susan jumped onto the shoulders of the other leaning against the wall trying to catch her breath. In one smooth movement she had leapt up and grabbed onto the edge of the wall. Susan pulled herself up on to the wide top surface on the wall.

Glimpsing back towards the doorway, she saw one of the biggest women she had ever seen standing in brightly lit doorway. She was clearly an aboriginal Indians. The large woman was dressed in a blouse with purple slacks. She didn't move, she just watched carefully as Susan fought her way out of her domain. Carefully she seemed to be examining her opponent.

Suffering in pain, Susan crawled along the top of the wall for a while in total darkness as she had just lost her night goggle. She could just see the edges of the wall and the dark forest in front of her, as she fell forward over the wall losing her balance.

CHAPTER SEVEN

Elliot Lake—The mansion
11:45 PM

A tomblike silence permeated the frigid blackness of the cold-blooded garden. Littleone stood silently in the doorway glaring down at her beaten companions. *"Dogs",* she said. *"You let one small thief enter my domain and escape."* With that she statement, she closed the doorway. The freezing cold enclosed garden, with its' elevated granite walls would suffice to allow her companions to think about their failure. Darkness and silence prevailed, until moaning in pain, but too frightened to enter the mansion, they silently regained their footing in the snow.

These were tough, strong ladies who hadn't failed their master before. Anxiety filled their minds. Dread at their lack of success, alarmed them. Their master was a commanding figure. Littleone, a powerful woman with a quick temper had been provoked to rage. Whispering together, they agreed it was best choice to sit quietly in the snow, until commanded to re-enter the hugged ominous mansion. A dreadful fate would occur if they opened the door without her permission.

55

Half frozen, suffering from their bruises they dwelled the intruder's escape. Twenty minutes slowly passed by and still they sat starring at the closed door. Finally, Littleone opened the heavy creaking door and bid them come in. *"You have suffered enough, as I also have suffered great failure"* She admitted. Each of them with filled with shame for their failure, lowered their eyes and slipped by their leader into the warmth and light of the mansion.

"Come in my frozen pets" She snarled.

Waving a huge hand, she motioned towards four heavy blankets for them to wrap themselves in. *"Perhaps this time I have been too hard on all of you, come with me and I'll show you why."* Littleone said, as they followed her down the concrete steps. It was a dark stairway, but the steps were lit by small bulbs near the top of each step.

"The dark one has entered my house by the top of the gable roof through the skylights at the ceiling of the mansion. I never thought of the possibility, I should have had a better security system. I never thought anyone would have the gall to attempt to entry our mansion. She had stolen everything of importance in the safe. But mainly I fear also, my most treasured possession that I own." She declared." *Now is not the time for punishment, but to get back what is mine, and should never have been taken."* Littleone thought to herself, *I will be the disgrace of the* Female Suffrage *and Carrie if I cannot retrieve what was taken, and the disaster, it could cause our plans.*

Littleone was dressed impressively in a pressed white blouse with a rattle snake belt, grey dress pants and black shiny leather boots. Her sleeves were rolled up. The muscles of her forearm stood out. She was a large women standing approximately six feet tall. She had broad shoulders which stretched tightly her expensive blouse. Her hair was jet black and hung over her shoulders. Littleone was a gorgeous woman with a dark complexion like that of a golden sun before it lowers itself over the horizon. *"Now is not the time for punishment, you were dogs in my eyes, but having also having been disgraced myself, I know what you are feeling. All of us were dogs too have let this happen. But now I return you to wolves and myself to a grizzly bear."*

"Who amongst you volunteers' to track down this dark shadow, to seek out the path of this black spectre, report to me, and then await our arrival." Littleone said, as she sensed their uncertainly. Instead of waiting, she nodded towards one who seemed hurt the less than the others. "Climb *over the wall, follow her tracks, see where she goes and then call me."* Littleone stated. "Timber *Wolf, take what you need and go."*

Littleone was getting interested. It had been awhile since she had someone challenge her. Glancing at the next of her three final ladies, she grabbed her and lifted the large pre-maturely hair woman off her feet and said. *"Whitefeater, you will pay a visit on Ruth Tanner at the Bon Air Motel. See if she has returned. We need information, anything of importance. Find out if she was in her room tonight. Use any method you have to, short of killing, to get the manager and staff to tell us about her."* Looking her deeply in Whitefeater eyes, she told her. "Use *one of our cars, visit her personally, then call and report back here."*

"*Dancing feet, your assignment is to go up into our communication tower, and set up the necessary equipment to monitor all radio frequencies going out of Elliot Lake. Elliot Land is a small, isolated town with one main highway. I want you to call our special friends with the local Ontario Provincial Police, have them set up road blocks on the main access roads and back country roads. Make it look like the OPP are searching for impaired drivers. Tell them we have been robbed by a thief with a black eye patch. Her size is approximately five feet, six inches tall. She appears to be well built and from what I saw, moves like a cat.*" Dancing feet was puzzled about how her master knew so much information. She knew better than to ask as she left about her duties.

"*Mina Kaur, I consider you the smartest of my pack. You may stay here and assist me.*" Littleone looked at the last member of her gang. She had a slim but wiry build. Her black hair was always messy and a deep, ugly scar ran down one of her cheeks. "*You undoubtedly are wondering how I know so much about our little thief. I will take you into my confidence, but if you talk to the others . . . well forget about your job, your family and any of your friends.*" Cringing at Littleone' speech, howling 'white feather felt fear as she dwelled on what had just been told to her.

Two large strides took Littleone over to the pool racks holding the pool cues carefully arranged against the wall maps. From a container holding the striped and solid balls Littleone grabbed the black eight ball. "*Solid magnetite, it is a very powerful magnet.*" Taking the magnetic eight ball over to the map of the world, she held it up against the Province of Ontario, Canada. Obviously there was a steel plate under this area of the map, and the magnet's grip was almost unbreakable. Glancing up towards the top corners of the room, Littleone pointed at a round felt-like surface with a clear circle in the middle. "Cameras *and microphone*" Said Littleone, as she pulled on the magnetic eight ball opening a well concealed doorway leading into another room. "Very *expensive cameras, designed to see in the light or dark and record sounds into this room.*"

The room was large. It was a computer room, comfortably outfitted with the top of the line computer systems. The room was full of various size scanners and printers. "Watch *this.*" Instructed Littleone, as she set up the computer program specifically designed to record what went on in the room. The liquid plasma monitor showed in a glowing green, a women climbing down a rope and then almost losing her balance and then smoothly landing on the floor. The camera showed the women searching the room, opening areas on the wall maps and stuffing maps into her knapsack. It then showed her violating the safe and removing everything from it. It then went on to show her frantic escape, and Littleone and her ladies entering the room.

"Based *on what I have seen recorded, I know that she took specific maps of interest from two separated locations. I checked on this computer which has a scanned copy of each of the rolled up map along with any reports.*"

"*That property was called the Lachaise Property, and the mineral rights were owned and operated by a large Geology Company that does International Geological operations around the world. Either this thief is working for Ruth*

Tanner or she is Ruth Tanner. How she knew about our operation is beyond my comprehension. Someone dressed up like a thief knew enough to try and get back their valuable information about the property. Little does this thief know that all information has been scanned and stored onto this computer?" Lovingly she patted the computer.

"We *know the thief is corrected to Ruth Tanner, my male cats tell me that she is staying at the Bon Air Motel. Elliot Lake being a small town on a minor highway doesn't give her many ways of getting out or communicating with the outside world. Most importantly at the moment, I sent Flying Fish to track her trail quickly and see where it leads, Whitefeater job is to find out anything she can on Ruth Tanner, and Dancing Feet to see if her plans to escape Elliot Lake by car or airplane."* Littleone said as she looked at Mina Kaur.

Mina Kaur spoke up "*Very well thought out and said try and find where she goes tonight, more about her and if plans on leaving Elliot Lake!*" She thought deeply! "This *is a very unusual character we are dealing with, and I wondered what was in the safe! None of my business what was in the safe . . . , just trying to place myself in her position."* Mina Kaur rested against the scanner table.

"*This other woman is smart, probably wounded; I think she knows better than to go back to the Motel if that's where she came from. The roads are blocked and she will probably anticipate that move. As to our communication system she probably has no clue . . . I think that's our best bet. She has to hide out or get out. Possibly flying fish can track her into town and we get her there. If not, then at night there aren't too many ways out except by ski-duo to a neighbouring town like King Elliot. I think we should also put some of our friends in Larder Lake, King Elliot and Swastika. An alert for her robbery to the OPP and our male cats might not hurt if she decides to go into hiding in town."*

Littleone pondered deeply about the thief opportunities. What would she do? If the thief was Ruth Tanner, then one possibility struck her hard. A perfect place for a geologist to hide out would be on her property at the base camp. Perhaps she would stay at her base camp where her geological operations were in progress. What Ruth didn't know was that all of her line cutters and project people worked for Littleone. Everyday, they monitored her daily progress on the line cutting and geophysical exploitation. They had even found out, about the possibilities of a Kimberlitic Deposit, which could indicate the presence of future diamond mining.

"Mina! Send a message of possible visitors to them base camps at Lachaise, Bompas and Montpelier Properties that she is currently working on. Wait for flying fish to call in and report. When we know more the five of us can pay a visit to this dark thief. Also, call my dogs and tell them to keep a lookout for her. Leave me now, say nothing of this room, and tell me when we can move. "Littleone motioned with her hand for mina to leave.

As Littleone was left alone in the silent room, she pondered about her life and what she had to do now. The contents of the safe were invaluable. She hated what she had to do now, calling the Female Suffrage and reporting what had happened. She would be furious but better she found out through herself than by her spies. Not reporting in would be a painful death. After tonight she would contact her two Captains and then talk to Carrie about what had occurred here tonight. Fearfully, with deep dread and shaky hands she started dialling out on a special untraceable line to talk to the Female Suffrage. No answer!

Thank the mighty spirit gods above she thought. She would try calling again in the morning, she would have more information by then.

CHAPTER EIGHT

Elliot Lake, 11:45 PM
Friday Night

Downward into the silent darkness, a black shaped dropped towards the forest floor. From the icy surface of the granite wall, Susan fell ten feet towards an unknown surface. She landed with a crunching noise, on a mound of deep, hard packed snow. Slowly she lifted her head. Upwards the wall protruded with patches of rough granite and cement. Moving her head sideways, she noticed how lucky she had been. Susan had landed between a patch of stunted, malformed, yet very hard looking trees. She had missed them by about two feet away on either side. Had she landed either way the fall would have easily snapped her back.

Through a haze of moving shapes, which dazzled her eyes, she raised herself wincing at the pain on her right side. Moving slowly, she touched her body feeling for any broken ribs. None she decided, though it would hurt like hell in the morning. *Damn my snow suit is somewhere hidden on the far side of the mansion's walls*, she thought. Standing up she shook off the pain and limped into the densely packed trees, wading through the three foot deep drifts of gripping snow. Susan had to push hard, as she forced her way through trees twisted tightly with bushes and picky vines.

Listening she could hear her feet crunching in the frozen snow of the long driveway. Finally reaching the end on the driveway, she turned left and crept along the edge of the tree covered road. Turning around quickly, she thought she had sensed someone's presence. Probably nothing, but none the less she remained cautions. By her calculations, she figured it should take around twenty minutes of sneaking through the tree's shadows until she hit a side street. After that she would head towards the main streets of Elliot Lake.

Susan had decided not to go back to the Bon Air Motel. The people in the large house definitely had a handle on what went on in the area. They knew what people were staying longer than a weekend in Elliot Lake.

Great, just great, here I am clad in black army pants and a black winter army sweater. Not to forget the black hat, dark gloves and boots. Especially noticeable was her black eye patch. Susan thought to herself.

Do I risk going back to the Motel? No, it went against any training that she had taught herself. Hell, the way I feel right now I'm just going to walk straight down Main Street. She knew that the darkness wouldn't hide her easy and obvious trail, as they would probably be using flashlights to follow her.

No, there had to be another way to hide out for a while. Looking around, she saw that she was in a tougher section of town. All around were dingy restaurants, bars, pool halls and strip joints. Susan glanced upwards at a hanging sign creaking in the cold breeze. O'Heaphy Irish Sports Bar could barely be read through the pealing paint. *Looks as wretched, or as good as any other place in the neighbourhood, she figured.* She slipped into the dark, long entrance. Opening the stained glass door, she was stopped BT an extra large bouncer with muscles protruding from her tight t-shirt. The bouncer glanced at her attire and asked for her three dollar cover charge. The money covered the cost of the band playing the local Friday night entertainment. The bouncer didn't give her outfit a second look. Susan figured the bouncer had seen every type of character.

Inside was a rough crowd of miners who worked hard and dangerous jobs at the local mines. Town folk also came here seeking to let off a little steam, after a hard weeks work. The rowdy entertainment provided women and men, dancing, smoking, drinking and maybe the possibility of a good bar fight. *This Friday night had quite a crowd. Probably a good band playing and it's packed so fully no one can notice all of my clothing attire,* Susan decided.

She squeezed between groups people wedged together, most of them drunkenly voicing off at each other. The bar was divided into three large sections. A pounding band played their loud music in one large room. People danced to the beat of the "*The Twisted Oysters*" as the overhead banner showed the bands' name.

Another room had a section of twelve pool tables with people lined up to get their shot at the pool table.

Turning left, Susan entered another room with scantily clad males serving drinks. Meanwhile on stage, exotic dancers slowly and provocatively removed their erotic clothing to music they had chosen before they began entertaining the cheering crowds.

Normally, she would have never have entered the bar. It wasn't her thing. Tonight though, it was like she was drawn into the mood of the room. The crowd roared as a handsome, tall, muscular blond man, extremely well proportioned all over sauntered onto the raised dance floor. *Construction worker on weekdays she guessed, but most definitely a man worth watching.* She couldn't keep her eyes off him as he slowly removed his neck tie and shirt off to the drum roll. Well all eyes are on him she assumed, as she squeezed her way through the drunken weekend crowd. The crowd let out another roar as his pants fell slowly to the brightly lit glass floor.

Quickly she sat down in the corner at an empty table with her back towards the wall. Second nature for protection, but tonight she was enthralled by this muscular man with his amazing body. Though she found it hard to take her eye off him, she saw the occasional glance at her attire. They quickly turned away when they saw the hardened anger in her left eye. A few women in the crowd glazed lustily at her with her short, but well built body clad in her dark attire on clothing.

Adjusting herself in her chair, she stared up at the stripper on the raised dance floor stage. She was finding herself even more enthralled in his erotic body movements, as his clothing was tossed into the audience for keepsakes. At the ends of the stage were two brass columns reaching up to the ceiling. She forgot all her problems as she watched him lift his naked body up the brass columns with his arms caressing the cool metal.

She sucked in her breath as she watched him flip his body upwards, using the strength in his legs to hold himself upside down. He then spread out his arms towards the crowd. Slowly he lowered himself downwards onto a bearskin rug lying below. The crowd moaned as he manipulated his body around the rug, and raised himself up as the song ended. Gathering the rug around his body . . . showing a few essential body parts. He smiled at the crowd and dropped the bearskin rug to the dance floor. Beer bottles fell out of the ladies hands. The crowd went crazy, roaring and raising what was left of their beer bottles to him as he descended the stairs and disappeared into the back room.

Receiving a soft touch on her shoulder, Susan shifted around in her padded chair and felt the air sucked out of her lungs. A young, vivacious, black man dressed in a black lingerie outfit had motioned to her, asking her what she wanted to drink. Susan felt like she was under a spell. This man was handsome in an exotic way. In the distance of her mind, she could hear him asking her what she would like to drink.

Susan, tried to speak, but was held spell bound by his lovely smooth face. He had individually, tightly twisted braids of hair which reached above his shoulder. His eyes were a shade of ocean blue. Jamaican earrings dangled from his earlobe, while an unusual, yet attractive, necklace combined of intermixed strands of coloured hemp and seashells hung around his slim neck. She forgot about the man, who was on stage, this one had a body that interested her even more. The young man wasn't tall, but he had a wiry, muscular body that ladies found sensual. Moving with a catlike motion he easily managed a full tray of drinks with one hand, avoiding the crowd of people by raising the heavy tray above his shoulders. His outspread fingers deftly managed to balance it.

Perceiving something in her that he likes, he lowered his mixture of drinks on the unwieldy tray onto her table. He offered her a cold bottle of beer as he sat down close to her. Susan placed the bottle over to the side of the table. He whispered in her ear so that only she could hear. *"You're not like the others in this bar."* He softly said. Gazing deeply at her, he examined her carefully. *"Something strange about you, I don't think that you are the bar scene type. Tell me about yourself."* He spoke with a voluptuous Caribbean Island accent which she didn't recognize, yet found she enjoyed. Susan, finally able to speak declared," *You're right, I'm not here for this type of entertainment; I don't usually hang around bars. Tonight, I'm trying to hide from people on the lookout for me."*

Raising himself up, he moved over seating himself comfortably on her lap. The young man stretched out his body and grabbed the back of her head. *He fells so silky, she noticed, as she gazed down at him up thrust chest, showing clearly from her vantage point,* she thought to herself. *"I have a talent for spotting out decent people, you may have some kind of strangeness to you but I think that I can tell down deep you are kind women, a lady if you will. You look totally out of place in here, but there is something about you that make me want to know you."* The young man stated.

Susan felt very uncomfortable. All of her life she had stayed away from men for some reason, but she felt attracted to this young, handsome man immediately. Her mind was blank, but her body was rising to the occasion.

Suddenly she heard a soft voice whispered in her ear. *"He is quite manipulating! eh, Ruth Tanner or whatever you call yourself."* Susan tried to stand up, but a firm, large hand held her down. *"Relax, you're amongst friends Ruth. What a time tracking you down!"* Grabbing a chair she yanked it over to join their table. Susan felt a huge grip, immensely strong, and a pat her on the back that pushed her forward. The strength in this woman seemed incredible. The young man on her lap paid no attention to the stranger, as he seemed to know her voice. He made himself move comfortable and moved Susan's hands onto his slim, muscular waist and moved her hands up towards his hairy chest, moaning with delight.

Susan turned her neck to the left, so that her good eye could take in the size of the women seated next to her. The woman is colossus, was her first thought. After taking a quick look at her, she soon felt herself turning back towards the exotic beauty snuggling up against her.

"Shark you leave her alone, I found her first" she said with her Caribbean accent. *"Don't mean her any harm."* Her soft voice thundered out. *"It's just that she was a hard woman to track down, ten years actually."* Word of warming though stay away from the guy on stage, he mine, but it seems that you found yourself a little bow to take care of you now."

"*Been a long time looking for you sister, my name is Alyssa Lawless.*" She growled. "*Or as my friends, call me shark.*" Susan, trying to see if she knew her, but no revelation struck her. "I *have no idea who you are or why you're calling me sister, you say you have been trying to find me. We can discuss your vivid imagination later, but for no sister, you're absolutely correct, right now I feel like the luckiest woman in the world.*"

Making a grand entrance from the backroom outfit changing area, the tall blond hulk strolled through the room. The crowd parted like the Red Sea. Obviously, He enjoyed the attention as he smiled and thanked people for their attendance. A rude comment came from a women in a chair seated in front of him. "*Hey, Ruth watches this.*" Susan pointed out the situation. Mack's smile changed to grimace. It always had to happen. He reached over and grabbed the edge of her shoulder squeezing hard. "*What did you say?*" He replied as the woman's face reddens. This was no ordinary blond, she realized, as the pain intensified. She could take it, it hurt too much." *Sorry, shouldn't have said what I did.*" She answered back. Releasing her, he smile broadened and he shook his long blond hair and headed towards the back wall.

"That's *my babe, strong, pretty and smart and he sure can handle himself.*" Alyssa looked at Ruth, who nodded appreciatively? Like an actor, his mannerisms and acting were second nature to him in this bar. The audience expected it. Smoothly he smile changed from a fake look to look to one of anticipation. He came over and dropped himself onto Anne's lap. "How's *my big beautiful of a lady. Noticed you made a new friend. Where'd you pick her up at in an army surplus store?"* He laughed at his joke. "Shame *on you Kevin, who is the good looking lady you're sitting on or maybe turning on."* He laughs out. His laughter was infectious and soon he had them all roaring away laughing. The men obviously knew each other and chatted away.

Susan didn't normally drink, but she pulled a glass of red wine off the tray and passed it to Anne and took a fresh one for herself. The other glass of wine, left untouched sat at the other side of the table. She touched her glass with the big lady beside her and sucked back the entire glass of roseate wine in one gulp. *"Never drank before in my life or a lot of stuff that's happening tonight, but the occasion seems right. Have to say, much better. My name is . . . ."* Susan hesitated, she didn't know these people. Should she follow a group of strangers? It went against her rules that she had lived by for all these years. A minute went by while she studied each off them." *I trust the three of you, I guess my name at the moment is Susan Gardener; normally I go by the name of Ruth Tanner. It changes when needed or I feel different. Anyways, I take it this hulk on me is Kevin, but who is your friend on your lap."*

Instead of waiting for Anne to introduce him, he said in a husky voice *"Mack, no nicknames, false names or made up names for me."* Anne reached over and passed him another beer. This time she touched Susan glass against her and said. *"Isn't life great right now?"*

The ladies soon turned their attention to the guys seated on their laps. Soon they were deep in conversation with their partners. After some intimate conversation,

Susan began talking to Anne, while holding firmly on to Kevin waist. She wasn't prepared to let this one get away.

It was slightly difficult for Susan to look at Anne and not be able to see Kevin at the same time. Realizing her handicap, Anne adjusted her chair in front and slight to the side. All the time making sure she didn't lose her comfortable position with Mack.

Susan soon realized that this giant stranger Alyssa Lawless, or Anne as she preferred, had been hanging around Elliot Lake for quite a while.

Approximately the same time period Ruth Tanner, her usual character, had been exploring the various geological properties that she owned in the area.

Kevin, who seemed to be very intuitive, sensed Susan's clumsy and awkward attempt at conversation with him. *"My serving name is Kevin, I don't tell anyone my real name because I don't want them coming onto me and starting to harass me."* He leaned over her ear and whispered his real name to her. *"Nice name, hard to pronounce, but still very pretty."* She declared back to him. Kevin told her that he believed in first impressions of people, how he could feel sensations about them." *At this time I get the impression that you live the lives of two different people, but I don't care. I feel comfortable and safe with you."* Kevin said as he cuddled up against warm clothing.

Susan looked at him closely, studying his eyes and her sense told her that he was expressing emotions that were difficult for her. *"You really do like me? I'm not a feminine in fact I've never gone out with a man before and it's new for me. Kevin, I felt something the moment I glanced into your eyes. I'm a very complex person, dangerous to be around; do you want that in your life? This may be a little quick, but that's the way I am.*" She said, as she continued looking deeply in his eyes. Would you come away from this place and start a new life with me somewhere else? Susan shyly asked. "*Yes, I want more in life than serving drinks to horny and frisky old dunks and hell yes . . . I would love to start my life over with someone who cares about me.*" Kevin stated.

A tear ran from his eyes, down his dark cheeks onto her sweater. "*It hasn't been easy for me, my parents moved up here Anguilla in the Caribbean's, they died when I was sixteen and I've had to do terrible things to keep myself alive for the last three years.*"

Susan held him tight, "*My life has been a tough one also, I have no memory of my youth, went to school for geology . . . but I'm also at times a thief. There, it's out. By the way, I can easily make our lives together very comfortable since I have more money than I know what to do with.*" Susan snapped back. "*I don't care about your money, just you! Although, I'm not saying that's bad thing.*"

Susan looked at him and told him. "*I haven't had a boyfriend before, we could try . . . if you like . . . you'd be the first.*" Kevin cuddled up more and talked into her sweater.

"*Oh, please let it be me . . . I saw something in you at first glance, mystery, adventure and hopefully something permanent between us.*"

Still on the alert for danger, Susan could see a disturbance at the entrance of the O'Heaphy Irish sport bar with her good eye. It was the four aboriginal Indians that she had fought

73

with a short period before, followed closely by a huge women Kevin said. "That's Littleone Whitefeater and her followers, now I know why you are hiding out here." It was the same woman she had noticed in the mansion's entrance before she had tumbled over the granite wall. They had tracked her down. In the darkness of the corner, Anne's huge shoulders blocked her from sight. They hadn't noticed her yet.

"Anne, take care of the guys, a storm is rolling in." She then turned to Kevin and Mack and said. *"Hold this knapsack, hide and guard it. Try not to let anyone get it. Don't look into it for your own good. Whatever's in it, those big aboriginal Indians over there will be hunting it down and I assume kill for it."* Quickly she turned to Kevin saying." *Not to late to change your mind about me, danger always follows me. Do you still want to know me?"* He nodded his head, looked over at the entrance and said." *Littleone, very dangerous, you do make friends. Yes, I still want us together."* She passed him a cellular phone and her business card said. *"Well I know her name now; I have an extra phone always. Call this number as many times as it takes to track me down and I'll get back to you."*

Silently, with great anger at being disturbed, she slid into the darkness of the room, using the furniture and the people to mask her appearance. The aboriginal Indians were near the edge of the dance floor in the other room blocking her escape. If they want to play the game, I can play it just as hard she thought.

Kevin and Mack pushed at Anne to go help Susan, who seemed to be trying to cross the dance floor towards the pool tables with its twelve tables neatly lined in a grid pattern. Downing another wine, she looked the scene over.

Kind of curious what her plans, anyways you stay put and watch the knapsack. It seems to be important to Susan or Ruth, whatever her name is. I'll just observe her for a moment; keep an eye out to make sure that they don't play dirty. I'd like to see her in action, see if she is as good as I think before I get involved."

"*Kevin, you really like her, she's not too much for you . . . ?*" Anne asked as he nodded his head." *Mack, what about you, if you want to get involved with me. I'm in the same boat as Susan, there's an attachment between us that I can tell you about later. I can only promise you an uncertain life, one that is full of trouble, danger and adventure. Maybe you both should think it over. Mack, you have my cell number, you can call me or whatever her name is.*"

"*Keep an eye on her for me would you? I have to place a quick phone call.*" Anne rumbled. With her, sausage like fingers, she pressed the tiny numbers on her miniature blue coloured cell phone. She looked over at the two men and then placed her attention back to concentrating on her call.

The phone rang, and continued to ring . . . and it seemed like no one at this hour of the night would answer." *Exactly what would you like Anne; I'm sort of occupied at the moment.*" The voice was high, pleasant, but a voice capable of great volume and changing tone. "*Kelly, good to see you have a call display finally . . . I can hear from that sweet giggling in the background that you're still on top of things, so I'll make it quick.*" Anne thundered out with her unusually, loud voice." *I found her, Ruth Tanner, strange character, here in Elliot Lake, right in our Province, but it's a long story. She seems to call herself Susan Gardener also. Yeah, okay, right, you call the girls and we'll meet at your place at the Chateau Laurier Hotel in two days. Rooms reserved at this time. We'll all let you take care of the bills; don't forget how rambunctious we are when the gang get together. Oh, bye the way would you reserve a couple of extra rooms just in case. I'll even let you pay the bill. It sounds to me like I called at the wrong time, but not a bad time for you. Tell him I'm sorry for calling this late and Kelly don't do anything I would do."*

Anne looked over at the guys and cautiously said. *"That was Kelly Macdonald, our . . . leader, in case you're curious. She told me to call her the exact moment that I was sure when I found Ruth. Although, I think I caught her in a different sort of position."* The men looked at her, laughed and wondered what the hack she was talking about. Who was Kelly Macdonald? Looking over at the dance floor, Anne stood up, stretched out her large girth and gave both guys a kiss on the forehead. *"It's time to see how Susan is doing and I'm itching for some action. As I always say, once in a while you just need a good workout."*

Susan removed her black toque and let it held it in drop to the floor. She pulled off her black eye patch over her head and held it in her hand. Seeing a tall brunette guy dancing alone on the dance floor, Susan reached over and grabbed his hand. *"Feel like dancing?"* She asked. He looked her over at her and she could barely hear him as he said." *Sure, I'm Mitch.* "Using a charm that she didn't realize she was capable of, she whispered in his ear." *My name is Joanne, let's swing over to this edge of the dance floor, there more room.*" Susan had never danced before in her life but she had agility, grace. Watching closely at what the other dancers were doing, she soon matching, if not improving on their style of dancing.

What a night she thought, why on earth did I never go out like normal ladies and have fun like this. Men galore and this dancing thing weren't that bad either. Good looking guys this Mitch. She felt bad about using him to get to the other side of the dance floor undetected. It was important to reach the edge of the dance floor and mix in with the crowd before she was detected. Susan was trying to draw the attention of the Aboriginal Indians away from her new friends and the precious knapsack that she had worked so hard to obtain.

Mingled in the crowd were several large muscular bouncers wearing black t-shirts. The shirts were inscribed with a white inscription depicting the name of the bar. They all wore tight blue jeans and running shoes.

Suddenly, Littleone with her large height noticed Susan. Pointing towards her, she said." *That one, she has taken off her eye patch and toque but her outfit gives her away. Flying fish surround the dance floor and let us remove her from this place.*" Mitch was enjoying Susan erratic movements, as she tried to get off the dance floor. She assumed that this was her style of dancing.

Everyone around was getting into watching them, yelling them on. *Not good* thought Susan, as she saw the Indians surrounding the dance floor. Meanwhile the space around Susan and the good looking Brunette, she was dancing with, was opening up, so that people could watch the two dancing. Littleone stood watching to make sure that Susan couldn't escape.

"*Mitch, go down quick.*" Susan shouted. "*Wow, already.*" He said as he lowered himself down. "Naughty boy, she thought. Howling' Flying fish leapt at her from the edge of the dance floor. Ducking down, Susan twisted her body to the right, using Howling' Flying fish weight to grab her and flipped her hard onto the wooden floor. Hurriedly, she put back on her eye patch, feeling the strength that it gave her. A disappointed Mitch moved over to the edge of the group of people. Littleone' ladies were leaping in, while the bouncers hurried to prevent a fight.

It was too late; a large burly miner with a long scraggly beard grabbed one of the Indians and one of the bouncers and smashed them together. Soon the dance floor had become a bedlam of furious fists. *It sure doesn't take much to start a rumble near two AM in the morning. Especially at closing time, Susan thought.* Twisting her body catlike, she edged her way through the turmoil the edge of the dance floor.

The drunken crowd in the other rooms soon kicked. The exotic dancing room and the pool hall soon started a major bedlam. Mack and Kevin watched from the back wall of the exotic room. The fighting seemed to be everywhere; people were bound to get hurt or worse. As a large woman was shoved towards Mack, she grabbed the back of her coat collar and her belt and easily tossed her into a group of people. Mack's muscles weren't just for looks; she did the same underground mining as the men with the heavy tools and machinery. She was almost Amazonian in her strength.

"Did you see Susan dancing with that guy?" Kevin said with a jealous, yet sad look. *"You twit, she just used him just to get off the dance floor."* Mack let loose on Kevin." *Sorry didn't mean to talk to you like that, grab that knapsack and let's get out of here."*

A group of men approached Mack and Kevin. They started to grab onto them, trying to take the knapsack away even though they didn't have a clue what was inside. Smaller Kevin proved that he had a wiry strength and used his free arm to smack his elbow into one of the men's face. Then he brought the back of his fist into the men ear. Mack assumed a football stance of which she had played frequently. She dove into the group of men bowling them over. Littleone watched the incident from where she stood. Her stance was like one made of stone. She now knew where her possessions were. First, the thief, then later, it would be time to retrieve her possession from these men.

Susan, swinging her fists and charging through the crowd soon found herself in the pool room. *Not good, she thought, no exit out of here.* From the left side of her face, she could see four aboriginal Indians following her into the room. Inside were twelve huge, well maintained pool tables with about four foot spacing between them. The pool table was aligned three across and four down she notice. She leapt up onto the edge of the first pool table, she approached. *Just an hour ago, I was jumping off one,* she remembered. Narrowly, she missed being smacked by a strongly swung pool cue as she jumped upwards. Susan kicked out one of her legs into the face of her attacker, while still in the midair. Mina Kaur screamed in pain.

Moving quickly, Susan leapt over to the next table and then to the third table.

Flying fish, Dancing feet and White tiger followed her around the pool tables trying to trap her. Susan reached down into her side pants, with their large side pockets. She tended to use them to hold her various weapons and supplies that she occasionally found useful. She pulled out a viscous black knife. Shape on one side and serrated on the other, a throwing knife. Flicking the knife with a loose, but well aimed shot, Susan drove it into, White tiger's lower thigh. Two down, but still the other two Indians came on as she starting reached for her club like weapon located on her belt.

Susan was pushed down hard onto the table. Before flying fish or dancing feet could pin her correctly to the table she did a quick upward leap. This move brought her from her back on the table, up onto the toes of her feet. Using her right hand to hold her club, she flicked it expertly at dancing feet's head knocking her down. The heavy ball sprung itself back into position.

Anne entered the room calmly, hearing Susan yells out. "*That one was for Kevin.*" Rolling forwards down the table, placing her hands outwards, she spun herself in the air like a gymnast. Catlike, she landed with her legs outspread, and her arms stretched outward. Like lighting, she shoots out her whip like club. Striking like a cobra, it wrapped itself around one of flying fish's legs. A good yank and flying fish was swung backwards, striking her head against the edge of the pool table. "*That one was for Mack and Mitch.*"

Anne approached the table. Susan was reaching down with her hand on the edge of the pool table, leaping softly to the floor. *"Ouch, damn that hurt."* Anne confusedly exclaimed. *"What hurt?"* She asked Susan. *"Just got a paper cut on the edge of the table, and it hurts like hell."*

"Anne trouble at 180 degrees, large, huge and running at us at full tilt." Susan worriedly stated. Littleone seeing the damage to her ladies dodged between the tables, quickly approaching. Littleone approached said. *"Get out of the way fat, ugly white women."* Alyssa swinging her left fist in a powerful roundhouse hit meant to take out Littleone said. *"With a nose like that I wouldn't be talking about other people!"* At the same time Littleone swung out her huge left fist at Alyssa. A loud crack was heard as both fists crunched into each other at the same time.

Pandemonium ran wild as the bar fight continued. The local Ontario Provincial Police had just entered, but couldn't contain the out of control crowd. It was a large bar, with separate rooms, yet it seemed that within each room hell had broken loose. Miners, forest workers, mechanics who enjoyed nothing more than a weekend drunk were tying into it with the bouncers, town folks and anyone standing too close. People were pushing and shoving. Fist fights were breaking out and people were starting to get hurt.

The small group of Police who had first entered was merely a trickle in the bucket. As they arrived in, they had expected a small local bar brawl. They did not expect chaos let loose. Customers began a wild charge out the front and back entrance. It was like a pack of wild animals let loose.

Kevin and Mack watched on from where they were standing. All they could see was devastation occurring. They had just finished fighting their own skirmish. Kevin could not help but notice a large aboriginal Indian, with a hooked shaped nose, handsome features and long black hair watching them. The women stood head and shoulders above the rest of the people. She appeared to have watched the fight and how they clung tightly onto the knapsack. She had an evil look of satisfaction on her face. She then turned and followed Susan into the next room.

As the crowd poured out of each entrance like a river of water, Mack pushed Kevin against the wall to protect him the throng of people. Both were still dressed in silky outfits and were unsure as to follow the crowd out into the freezing cold weather. *"Do you think we could make it to our apartment dressed like this? It's about ten minute walk and it's cold out there."* Kevin asked Mack. *"Let's just wait here, we haven't done anything wrong and when the crowd thins out we can grab out clothes from the dressing room along with our jackets."* Replied Mack!

As she was speaking she noticed the large man walking slowly towards them. He was holding one of his hands painfully in the other as if he had hit something hard. The room was starting to thin out and the Police weren't inside the bar. They must be attending to the wounded at the front entrance. The men's backs were up against the wall. They knew that their combined strength would do little against a woman of her size. The back entrance was close but with their position they would be cut off by her approach.

Desperately they looked around at the few people left fighting in the room. *"George!"* Mack screamed out. She was yelling at the large gruff looking miner, who had basically started off the fight. He glanced over at the girls, took another large swing at those still standing around him watching as they toppled over like dominoes. George walked towards them. He was now between the aboriginal Indian and the girls. *"Hey Mack,"* Poured out a gruff voice.

The miner had on a thick green jacket opened up to show a red patterned woollen shirt underneath. He was a huge man. The part of his face that could be seen was heavily wrinkled with age and hard work. He was the only man in Elliot Lake to have worked underground at the original six famous gold mines in the *"Golden Mile"* as the area was known. His grey unkempt beard hung down low past his chin and his balding shaggy hair curled away from his head. He was tough as nails gold minor, who worked at the deepest mining levels. Mack worked at the same mine as he did and they all called him *George* because he was hard and tough. Yet he had a soft heart and treated friends good. *"George helps us!"* Pleaded Mack! Pointing at the approaching! Man coming towards them. *"He's after us and wants something that we have."* She continued.

The miner turned around and looked at the large Aboriginal Indian approaching them Littleone fixed an evil eye on the miner. *"Here girls, you must be cold, take this jacket and my heavy shirt and put them on."* George said, as he passed them his jacket and shirt. He eagerly turned towards the large man approaching them about ten feet away. Littleone looked at the old man, but didn't take him for granted. He could see a lifetime of hard work in the deep mines had made this man one not to be reckoned with. Littleone wasn't scared, but she was impressed by the huge bulk of the man who stood slightly shorter than her, but probably outweighed her.

The miner had deep scars on his large arms showing from his white short sleeved undershirt. Littleone's hand was painfully hurting at the moment. She was angry at the way the quick punch had smashed into her fist. "*Get out of the way old man.*" Snarled Littleone! *George* brought his face up close to that of Littleone "*Old man, eh! Think your tough going after two men, just wait until you buckle down with a gold miner.*"

At the moment as tension was about to erupt between the two of them more police poured into the bar. Littleone looked into the eyes of the old man and said." *For what you have done, your death will be a most painful one. I will personally take care of it and make you scream for me to kill you.*

Backing away, he added looking at the men. "*The old man, the one you call George, the one you have condemned to die, is right. It is not my job to attack women. As I have my wolves for hunting. I also have my cats for assignment such as this spread around town. You can expect a visit from my main man Black Panther. He'll spread the word to his cats probably Snow Leopard, white tiger and many more.*"

Turning to leave, he tossed into their worried faces. "*Many, many cats patrolling my town, Jaguar, Loin, Lynx,*

Cheetah, Bobtail, Cougar, Ocelot and many other forms of cats all over town. No I wouldn't want to be you. Hand over the knapsack and I'll call them off and your friends will not suffer needlessly. My wolves are tough, but my cats are another story. They are vicious and like cats, they like to hunt and play with their food before they eat it. Your lives are forfeit as of this moment and there is no place safe for you."

Getting angry, George swung at Littleone, who bent over with the sheer thrust of the punch. George pulled the guys out of the way, covering them with his huge girth called over to the police. Littleone was losing it now. This wasn't her style. Changing directions with a quick surprise turn, she ran at the policeman. Spreading out her huge arms she took out two unsuspecting policeman. She hit them so hard, that their legs flew out from under them and they landed hard onto their backs. Two more policemen launched themselves at her. She merely spread out huge hands, grabbed them by their necks and lifted them up in the air. She tossed them hard as she could at the remainder of the policemen knocking them over the floor.

Before she left the front door, she looked at George and made as if to slit her throat. Littleone then glanced at Kevin and Mack and said, "I hope my cats don't finish you off, after they toy with you both, my men would love to relieve some tension on the two of you and probably call in some friends. In the end you will personally and gladly handover that knapsack to me. A policeman lifted his head and Littleone gave him the smack down and beat him until he was raw.

Glancing at them, he added. "Wouldn't want to be you, three. It's time to get to work, so many people to kill and so little time to enjoy it." Like a Littleone Whitefeater in the night he melted into the dark of the outdoor evening.

"Police, get out of here!" Someone yelled! A fury of people, like a stampeding herd of cattle, raced towards the front entrance and back entrance as the police tried fruitlessly to bring back order to the chaos. Anne and Susan had been separated from Littleone by a wave of people hurrying between them, shoving both parties aside. Quickly, Anne grabbed Susan by the arm and pulled her towards the entrance. Littleone was no where to be seen. *"Wait, there's the coat check area." Alyssa told her as she shoved the door open and pushed a fur coat into Susan's arms.*

They race out of the building along with the throng of people pushing their way outward. "See what you did tonight by starting to drink wine and chase men." Happens to me all the time, but now you're blacklisted from the bar. Alyssa bellowed out as they both raced down the street and around the first corner that they saw. Peeking around the corner they didn't see anything suspicious. *"Well I hope that the guys got out safely. We can't go to Bon Air Motel, I'm known there and you . . . well, you're probably known all over Elliot Lake."*

Susan appeared lost in thought and said." *Anne, do you think that Kevin really like me? I haven't had much . . . well any experience with men, but I think there's something special about him . . . he could be my first boyfriend."*

They soon approached the buildings lining Government Road East and started crossing over Station Road. Susan reached through the folds of her fur coat, into her black pockets and pulled out a powerful mobile two way radio. Holding the transmitting button she said. *"Pick up required at BC, baseline 0*00 at 6 AM at Bompas*

Property, if we aren't there meet us south of the Airport, near the Ontario Northland Railway off Airport Road." A tried voice came back chuckling *"Susan that Susan."* Laughing at his, own joke.

"Well Anne, nearby at one of the warehouses I'm sure I have a couple of ski-duos, tonight we'll stay over at my Bompas property base camp that I'm presently doing geological exploration on. "Susan then added, *I'm sure they'll call."* as she spoke on *"We'll be perfectly safe there and we can get good nights sleep. If the guys need us I'm sure they'll call."* Anne looked at her. *"Sound like a plan, hope your friends have lots of food to eat, I'm starved and tomorrow we'll sleep in all day safely and not have to worry."*

With that they headed out towards the warehouse district of town. Thoughts of the guys, the action of the night and sleeping safely in comfortable, warm sleeping bags went through their minds as they headed out towards the warehouse. Someday they would be secure, with no worries. Base camp, located deep in the North forest area of Elliot Lake sounded like a great idea.